Christmas in Wylder

by

Sarita Leone

The Wylder West

Christmas in Wylder

Cover Art by *Tina Lynn Stout*

The Wild Rose Press, Inc.
PO Box 708
Adams Basin, NY 14410-0708
Visit us at www.thewildrosepress.com

Publishing History
First Edition, 2021
Trade Paperback ISBN 978-1-5092-4012-8
Digital ISBN 978-1-5092-4007-4

The Wylder West
Published in the United States of America

Dedication

For Vito Leone.

Eleven Christmases later
and I still miss him every single day…
because love never dies.

Acknowledgments

With sincere gratitude to Nicole D'Arienzo, Laura Strickland, and Kim Turner for embarking on this wonderful Wylder adventure with me. Writing a series within a series was a blast because of the three of you and the camaraderie we share. Thank you for making this one of the best experiences of my writing career. I am so grateful to be one of the Wylder Women!

Prologue

December 14, 1880

Derek Toliver didn't feel the cap fly from his head. If he lived past this snowstorm, he might lose his ears and maybe even his nose. Hell, he might've already lost them, for all he could tell.

A futile attempt to see what lay ahead by looking out into the storm anyway. Darkness fell, snow swirled, and the rumble of wheels rolling over icy track made discernment impossible. He should be nearing Wylder but how close they were was anybody's guess.

He'd lost track of both time and place several miles back. Now he prayed to get the train to the frontier town in one piece. If they made it he planned to stop for the night. Laramie could wait until morning.

Better to arrive than become one of the Union Pacific's casualty statistics. This close to retirement, his determination to leave without incident never wavered. So he prayed. And when he realized keeping his head out in the cold didn't do any good, he pulled it back inside.

And that, the moment he changed positions, turned out to be the one that claimed his life—and his engineer's clear track record.

He flew forward and his face slammed into the metal struts surrounding the side window. Bone and flesh became one sticky mess in a painful instant. He screamed but choked on the sound—his teeth sucked into his throat with his final inhale.

Glass shattered around Jake, the fireman, as he catapulted through the front glass screen and disappeared into the snowy vortex. Coal from the tender shot through the air into the engine's cab.

Satan, prying open the bowels of hell and inviting them in, couldn't have made more horrific sounds. Steel and iron split apart, turning the air into one unending screech.

For miles they'd battled the wall of white, hoping to bring the tons of freight, train cars, and human cargo traveling under their care safely to their destinations. Now it became clear that wouldn't happen.

In the seconds before his world went black, Derek imagined he heard cars tumbling off the tracks.

His heart stuttered, then stopped, and his world went silent.

Behind him, the chaos continued.

Chapter 1

Tate dragged the last wooden crate along the wagon bed, cursing his frozen fingertips as his grip slipped and nearly sent him tumbling backward into the snow. Muttering a word not fit for female ears, he grabbed the rope handle, closed his fingers tightly around the icy jute, and tugged it to the edge of the bed.

He jumped down off the wagon. Snow covered his legs to his thighs. Wet, white flakes fell so fast and blew so hard he could neither see nor breathe. He followed the tracks he'd left hauling the other boxes into the building, his feet fitting into the cavities they'd already made.

The back door stood open and a white carpet covered the wooden floorboards for a good five feet. Now he stumbled inside, hitched a foot around the edge of the door, and laid his back against it to close the weather out.

Piles stood around the snowy entrance, so he placed this crate on top of the nearest stack and rubbed his hands together. Damn, but his fingers felt like icicles!

A fire roared in the hearth out front, so he crossed the floor, his bootheels echoing, and entered the portion of the building facing the street. Separated from the back, this large room would do nicely for what he had planned. He stood beside the fire, held his hands toward the flames, and surveyed the space. In his mind's eye he saw wooden shelves holding miner's hats, hooks on the far wall for shovels, axes, and the like, and lanterns hanging from the exposed beams. A sales counter ran along the back wall out here. Picturing himself standing behind it, ringing up transactions and advising newcomers about the industry, he smiled.

It hadn't come easy to him, nothing in life had, but this realization of a dream almost made him forget the journey that led him here.

Almost. Nothing could entirely erase the hardship, misguided intentions, broken dreams, and damaged heart already come to him in his short time on earth.

But this? It felt good.

Taylor's Mining Supplies. He'd find a sign maker and have the man construct something respectable to hang above the front door.

Respectability. If only Father could see him now and know that despite having taken a few wrong turns on the road of life, his youngest son had made his way back to becoming a productive member of society. He'd be proud…if he were alive, that is.

Shaking sad memories from his head, Tate went for a broom to sweep the snow out of his back room. He didn't need any warped floorboards.

The mess had already begun to melt so he swept up what he could, opened the door and sent it out into the storm, then dropped burlap bags onto the area to absorb the water. He walked over them a few times, hoping his weight helped soak up the worst of it.

He'd never owned a building, hadn't thought it possible for a wandering war veteran who couldn't make up his mind about what to eat for dinner, let alone how to spend the rest of his life.

Tate arrived in the Wyoming territory with a dream to capture the heart of the woman who'd saved him when he lay dying but, as with the rest of his dreams, it got dashed to bits. Violet Bloom, Wylder's schoolteacher, had already lost her heart to local financier Thomas Harvey when Tate and Charles, his chestnut gelding, rode into town. His own heart cracked when he realized the truth. It had taken all his strength to ride away on Christmas Day two years ago. He knew she deserved to be left in peace but, damn, it felt as if he'd never find serenity of his own.

He stood the broom in the corner and went back to the front room to stand near the wide window. The view of Sundown Lane hid behind a wall of white. When the storm ended he'd see the other businesses that took hold on this side of the tracks. They mightn't be pretty, but they were necessary.

His mining supply stood right behind the Wylder County Social Club, a fancy name for the town's whorehouse. On his other side, a cabinetmaker. Next to that, the undertaker. All essential businesses, and each one benefitting of its proximity to the train tracks. Supplies came west on the Union Pacific. Better to be nearby rather than transport things miles over rutted lanes. Especially in his case, where explosives counted as inventory.

He should go unhitch the horses from the wagon and put both into the small barn behind the building, but he lingered a moment longer. He'd been on the move since before sunup and it had been one of those never-ending days. This moment of silence soothed his soul.

He'd been back in Wylder for three weeks and managed to avoid running into Violet. Truth be told, he and she didn't go in similar circles. And he'd spent most of the first weeks either tracking down a spot for his business or mulling it over with two fingers full of whiskey at the Five Star Saloon.

No way to avoid her forever, not in a town this size. Wylder had grown in the years he'd been out west, but it still didn't rival Charleston or Richmond. A pang of homesickness pricked his heart, but he swallowed hard and pushed it aside. No sense longing for the past—and that included delusions about life and love. No, best to belly up to the bar and take whatever hand got dealt with as much fortitude as possible.

He'd learned a few things in his lifetime. The most important, take the hit on the chin and stagger if you must but never, ever let anything or anyone drop you slid through his mind as he buttoned his jacket. A hook beside the back door held his hat, wet from snow melt but still better than nothing. He dropped the Stetson on and pulled it low as he stepped outside.

The building's covered back walkway made a good shelter for Charles. The horse stood still against the wall, as far in from the storm as possible. They'd crossed countless miles together and Tate could not imagine life without the smart animal by his side.

He went over and spoke softly. "Let me get the wagon horses in the barn. Then I'll come back for you and give you an extra long grooming. I only need a few minutes." He turned his collar up and took a step toward the wagon.

Charles nickered in reply. Then he flicked mane, an almost nervous gesture so out of character that

Tate turned back. He placed a hand on the horse's flank, noticing that it quivered. Something spooked the animal, but what? They'd been through bad snowstorms together, slept rough through some, and he'd never responded this way.

"Charles, I don't know what's going on in your head but whatever it is, lay it to rest. I promise, I'll be right back to get you bedded down." He leaned close and placed his forehead against the horse's. "We're in for new adventures, a lot better than some of the old ones. We've made it far without letting each other down. I won't let you down now. Give me ten minutes, tops, to get them unhitched and—"

An ear-splitting metallic groan tore through the silence, a noise so long and loud it might have been pulled straight from hell.

Horrific thumping noises and screeching that sounded like metal twisting and tearing apart followed.

The horse reared up onto his hind legs, came down hard, and danced on the wooden walkway. Tate grabbed the reins, leapt onto the saddle, and turned the animal around.

The commotion did not end. Crashing and squealing, interspersed by ground-shaking thuds, meant only one thing: The train due to pull into the station would not arrive on time.

If he guessed right, that very same train, even now, flew off the tracks.

Charles needed no encouragement. They cleared the wagon and tore into the street headed in the direction of what, most likely, held a horrific scene.

Chapter 2

Meg Channing loved long rides of any kind. Horse, carriage, stagecoach—they all gave her mind time to wander. Since her mother's passing, moments not occupied doing the Reverend's bidding were few, so any little escape lifted her mood and made her situation almost tolerable.

Almost. A small word that stood for a great deal.

She'd almost stayed behind in Boston.

Almost married the man her father, the very Reverend Simon Channing, chose for her.

Almost sold her soul to the devil himself, it felt like.

But this run for freedom, this long, slow ride across the country into what she hoped would be a fresh start offered hours for contemplation.

The Reverend insisted his daughter and wife spend several hours each day in quiet meditation. On their knees on hard floorboards in an unheated room. Without speaking. Sometimes, breathing too loudly brought the man's sturdy leather belt strap down across their shoulders.

Oh, yes, he'd encouraged a wandering mind—as long as it went in directions he believed suitable. She wondered how he knew what she contemplated but dared not ask.

There were too many unpleasant consequences

associated with questioning the man. There had been times since the fire that burned acres of the city and took her mother's life when she felt relieved for the woman who birthed her. The conflagration saved her from a lifetime of the Reverend's abuse.

And this train provided escape for the daughter left behind.

Meg looked at the woman opposite. They met in Chicago when Georgina boarded and inquired about the seat. She'd said no one claimed it, so the newcomer stowed her bag on the shelf above them and sat.

They became instant friends.

The other woman's head bobbed when the train swayed. She'd fallen asleep with a book in her hands an hour or so ago, and since the silence suited her, Meg did not wake her. Now she opened her eyes, dashed a hand beneath her nose, and yawned.

She blinked twice, giving Meg the impression she traveled alongside a beribboned, bespectacled owl.

"How long have I been dozing?" Her Italian accent turned the question lyrical.

"Once again, I love that accent. I wish I spoke the way you do." She heaved a sigh, knowing that she would never be as alluring as her new friend. They were a study in contrasts: one raven-haired with an olive complexion and eyes so dark they looked like the night sky and the other an alabaster-skinned blonde with light blue eyes. "And not long at all. An hour, maybe a little bit more."

She tucked her journal into the large floral-patterned satchel sitting on the floor between her feet. All her life she'd wanted a place to write her thoughts but had been too frightened to do so. If the Reverend found a journal there would surely be hell to pay.

Now, she did as she pleased. And she planned to keep on doing so.

Damn the Reverend.

He'd killed her mother, but she'd fight with every ounce of strength she possessed before he'd get her, too.

Georgina turned a page corner down on her copy of *Pride and Prejudice* and held it out. "Here, why don't you take this? I've read it several times already and I have another of hers in my bag. I've seen you looking at it, so please, take this one."

The Reverend judged women reading a vanity and he did not abide it under his roof. Aside from the Bible, which she could recite from cover to cover, she had read almost nothing else. Now she eyeballed the proffered Jane Austen with a hammering heart.

Did she dare?

"Are you sure? If we become separated in Laramie I may not be able to return it to you. I don't believe I can be that bold, to borrow a book without certainty of its finding its way home." Trepidation traced a finger up her spine. She wanted desperately to read it but could not put years of sermons aside.

The Reverend didn't believe in borrowing. She heard him in her mind, bellowing from the pulpit, "The rich rule over the poor. The borrower is a slave to the lender!"

Her new friend leaned forward and placed the book in her lap. "I insist. If we are separated—which I sincerely hope won't happen—I'll have faith that the volume has found a new home, and I will be happy for you, me, and Elizabeth, too."

She ran a fingertip over the spine. It seemed impossible that a novel she'd yearned to read had been given so freely. Her throat tightened and her eyes tingled. Since her mother's death, she rarely knew kindness in any form.

Meg met Georgina's gaze. "Thank you. I will not forget your benevolence, even if we do part in Laramie. But who is Elizabeth?"

The other waved a hand in the air between them. "Oh, you'll see who she is when you read the book. And I am sure you'll love her as much as I do." She dug into her bag and pulled out two apples. Handing one over, she said, "I believe we need a snack. There's no guarantee we'll find sustenance in the next stop—what is it again?"

She accepted the fruit with a smile and rubbed it against her skirt. Lanterns in the train car didn't illuminate much but habit made her shine the apple anyway.

"Wylder." She took a bite and chewed, loving the way the sweetness slid across her tongue. After she swallowed, she added, "In the Wyoming territory."

They both turned their gazes to the window. They'd heard it snowed but they could not tell. Darkness wrapped them in a cocoon that spread over miles, taking them to a destination that neither had seen. They did not know what to expect.

"Hard to believe we're nearly there." Georgina's cousin ran a boarding house in Laramie and had agreed to shelter her for as long as she wanted. "I hope my cousin isn't awful."

"How can you even think something like that? I bet she's wonderful. Imagine, offering you a home when you said you wanted to see the west." She took another bite and chewed thoughtfully. That must be how ordinary families did things. They sheltered each other because they shared a bloodline, not because anyone forced them to be kind. "I wish I had family, too."

She hadn't told anyone about her plan and didn't intend to, either.

Her mother had once said that women had to do whatever it took to survive. She'd meant putting up with the Reverend's whipping, but Meg hadn't forgotten—not the strap or the sentiment.

Now she planned to do whatever it took to keep herself alive—nobody's business save her own.

"You could come stay with me at my cousin's. I'm sure she has—"

A horrible screeching filled the air. The train car heaved, its front portion rising as if it intended to fly.

Meg flew from her seat. She fell forward, onto the other woman. They clung together as the world tilted.

Screams rang distant, background noise to the scraping of shearing metal. They hit something solid— so hard they both left the seat and were tossed into the aisle into a heap of tangled limbs.

She scrambled to her knees with the book still clutched in her hand. She stuck it in her bodice and grabbed for a seat to pull herself up, but the car lurched again.

It flipped and sent her crashing against what had been the ceiling. A lantern broke at the far end of the car and ignited the window coverings in a soft *whoosh*. She heard it because she'd blocked out the screaming and crashing sounds. For an instant she sat in the front pew looking up at the Reverend as spittle flew from his lips and he waved a finger toward the assembled, promising the wicked would get their due.

She'd gone against him and would be consumed in the fires of hell raging around her.

Meg covered her nose and coughed as smoke filled her lungs.

Time to settle up.

Chapter 3

Tate set out in the direction of the horrific noises, then gave the horse his head.

It made sense now that Charles had been so unsettled. Animals had a feel about things that humans did not, and in this moment he drew gratitude from that unique gift. Had he any idea that disaster loomed, he never would have been able to concentrate. He'd tuckered himself out, moving supplies into the building all day and into the evening, but a surge of adrenaline gave him energy now.

A train pulled into the Wylder station every Tuesday evening. This one carried holiday goods, as well as supplies to get townsfolk through the long, hard winter. He'd heard talk around town about gifts ordered from back east that would find their way beneath Christmas trees although now he doubted that any of the train's cargo would arrive in Wylder tonight.

It passed through his mind that if there was a wreck, as he suspected, the shipment he waited on might blow the whole place sky high.

A figure appeared on horseback to his right. Tate held up a hand to shield his eyes from the blinding snow and leaned close, trying to discern the rider's identity.

An unfamiliar voice called to him. "When we get there, look for cars where folks might be trapped.

14

Y'hear me? We gotta get people outta that train!"

He hadn't been born yesterday and if this weren't a catastrophic moment he'd remind whoever tried to school him of that fact. Instead, he shouted, "We should be close!"

Noise carries during a snowstorm so what sounded near might be farther than he thought. He hoped not. The weather turned uglier by the minute. People could freeze on a night like this, particularly if they were wounded from a crash.

The wreck appeared so suddenly Charles pulled up short. He snorted, tossed his head, and stamped. Clearly, the animal did not wish to go closer, so Tate jumped from the saddle and ran to the first car.

The engine lay on its side, smoke billowing from places it oughtn't be. He climbed over chunks of twisted metal, unidentifiable in the darkness, to reach the car. The undercarriage faced him, so he ran around the massive wall of steel to the other side.

Here, the front window had shattered. A charred body wrapped around the smokestack, beyond recognition, tendrils of smoke surrounding the form. Tate covered his nose against the smell of cooked flesh and stepped over the car's railing to access the cab.

The uniform gave the only hint to recognize who lay crushed against the side wall. The man's body remained intact but the same could not be said for anything above his collar. A bloody mass of hair, skin, and glass filled the space where his features should have been. Whatever he'd hit, he'd struck hard enough to pulverize his entire face.

Tate fought nausea, turning away as a man ran toward the engine car. He held up a hand and waved him back. "Nothing to do for the engineer. Fireman, either. We need to find survivors—if there are any."

He jumped down, glad to be away from the carnage. The heat from the crash melted some of the snow so he didn't sink deep which made it less taxing to run for the rest of the train.

Cars lay scattered like children's toys. Parcels, luggage, and bodies had also been deposited across a wide space.

Others were arriving, which gave him hope that they'd find survivors. The magnitude of the crash staggered him. Who knew how many passengers were trapped in the cars before them?

Worse, how many dead?

He'd seen death during the war but that did not compare to this. Wars occurred between armed men who were prepared to die for what they believed in. This train's passengers were innocent people. They did not bargain for their journey to end this way.

Shouts cut the night air. Other sounds, too. Groans. Anguished wailing. A crying baby, barking dog, screaming woman…they fell away like snowflakes when he heard sounds that made his heart stutter in his chest.

The popping noises, muffled by the snow and masked by the anguish, could have been any number of innocent things, but he knew better. He'd recognize the sound of gunfire anywhere.

Tate ran past the coal car, taking its scattered load like a goat clambering over a black mountain. Beyond it, two passenger cars. One crawled with rescuers. Men helped survivors from the wreckage while others led them toward safety, away from the debris.

16

The other car had flipped completely over. From the far end, smoke and flames shot from an open window. He saw two men attempting to kick in glass toward the front of the car. At the sound of popping from the carriage's interior, all three turned back. Glass blew out as the first window shattered. The pair hurried over and helped kick the glass aside to make an exit for those trapped within.

When they began pulling passengers out of the car, Tate continued toward the back. The smoke had turned thick and black, making it hard to see anything, but he felt his way forward.

Heat turned snow to slush and he slipped, slamming a shoulder against the unforgiving steel exterior. A spear of pain shot through him, up his thigh toward his gut. War wounds like his healed and while they might not kill they stuck around to torture a man for life.

He pushed to his feet, ignored the pain, and kept moving. People might be trapped in the fiery car. The only way to know for sure? Figure a way to get inside and hope that he'd find survivors instead of victims.

Chapter 4

It happened so fast Meg didn't have time to scream. One minute she and Georgina chatted about books. The next, they flew through the car's interior like dice tossed from an angry god's hands.

No line between joy and terror. No warning that their lives were on the brink of being lost to an awful twist of fate. No time to make amends for their sins, past or present.

It flashed through her mind that she deserved to die this way, without time to atone for what she'd done. This punishment for defying the Reverend had come by her own hand. Stubborn refusal to do his bidding would end her life and if the sounds of terror surrounding her weren't imagined, she managed to drag innocent victims along with her.

She must surely be destined to go to Hell as payment for this tragedy.

Georgina sprawled on her back with her eyes closed.

Meg glanced above. Rows of seats hung over them. The world had gone topsy turvy.

Her greatest fear made its presence known when the acrid smell of smoke reached her nostrils. Panic gripped her, sending every rational thought from her head.

Fire killed her mother, but it would not claim her,

too. She wouldn't allow it.

And it wouldn't get her new friend, either. She reached out and grabbed her by the wrists. She pulled her farther from the front of the car, away from the flames that slithered along seat cushions and over the bundles strewn about. A fiery snake, coming closer with every passing second.

Through the smoke she saw others climbing out windows.

Impossible to drag the other woman over the piles of luggage and debris separating them from the open escape windows without help. She had to find a way out on this side of the mess, and soon. Some smoke wafted out shattered windows, but most remained inside.

She covered her mouth and nose with one hand but that wasn't protection enough to stop her choking on the thick smoke. As she fought panic, she kicked a box beneath the nearest window and stood on it. She hammered a fist against the window above her. With the car on its roof, the panes were no longer accessible. The distance from the ceiling to the upper edges stretched beyond her reach but she jumped up and down, smacking the glass every time her fist drew close.

Her efforts were futile. The glass wouldn't break and even if it did, how could she expect to get the unconscious woman through the opening?

She squatted on the box, covered her nose with the crook of one arm, and searched for an alternate route out. The exit door a few feet away had been damaged in the crash but she ran to it and tugged on the handle. It didn't budge so she threw her body back, hoping to drag it open with her weight. Its twisted frame held it closed despite her best effort.

Time sped by. If she didn't find an escape in the next minute they would surely die!

She ran to Georgina. "Wake up! Please, wake up!"

The door crashed open behind her. A man dashed in. A bandanna covered the bottom half of his face, and he had a hat pulled low over his eyes but when he reached out a hand she took it.

"Come on—we've got to get you out of here!" His grip lifted her to her feet.

"W-wait—" The smoke choked her, sending her into a coughing fit that bent her double. The man tried to pull her into his arms, but she pushed him away.

"I'll carry you," he growled as he lifted her off her feet.

"No!" Her nose ran and her eyes streamed but she pointed over his shoulder. "My friend—she's unconscious. H-help h-h—" She gagged again, so violently she could not resist when he tucked her head against his neck and carried her out. Her eyes were closed but she felt him jump into the snow. She lifted her face to the cold air and gulped in breaths as he took her from the wreckage.

When he placed her on her feet she tried to run back to the train, but he grabbed her upper arms and held her in place.

"Stay here. I'll get your friend."

She watched him cover the space in a few strides. Smoke streamed from broken windows, but he did not hesitate. The stranger leapt into the overturned car and disappeared.

Meg had promised herself that she wouldn't pray

anymore, not once she'd left Boston and her nightmare life behind. The Reverend, with his harsh sermons and harsher punishments, cured her of wanting to ever talk with God again.

Now, she clasped her hands against her chest and opened her mouth, ready to break her vow if it might help save the two inside the train car.

While she struggled to find words, the man emerged with Georgina in his arms. She saw he limped and wondered if he'd been hurt but when he reached her he didn't give her a chance to ask.

"Can you walk?" The words came as a deep growl. When she nodded, he tipped his head toward the snowy debris. "Follow me. I'll get you out of here before you freeze."

Mayhem surrounded them but he strode through it all with military precision. Moving in a straight line proved impossible, with baggage, train parts, and people running about the scene, but his footsteps didn't falter.

There were people everywhere. Folks not dressed for the weather, looking as if they'd been roused from their homes, helping others move away from the tracks. Bloodied faces, an arm on a man dangling at a strange angle, and another being carried between two men. A woman stared toward the smoking cars, tears turning icy on her cheeks, her head whitened by snowfall. She thought to reach out to her but the man holding Georgina didn't slow so she passed the woman, offering a smile that did not get returned.

A big man strode through the snow with a child in his arms. Long, blond hair hung over the collar of his fur coat. His hat, also fur, had enough snow piled on it that he looked enormous. She glanced at the car he'd emerged from. It lay on its side, the undercarriage resembling a mechanical insect that had tipped over and had no chance of finding its feet.

He handed the youngster to another man and turned back to the wreckage as the little one called in a frightened voice for his ma. Her heart shattered as she wondered if the beloved mother was dead or alive.

She knew how it felt to be motherless. Tears gathered in the corners of her eyes, so she closed them and concentrated on stepping into the depressions in the snow made by their rescuer. Had they not been there she doubted she could have managed walking through the storm.

Suddenly he stopped and turned to her. When he met her gaze, she noticed that the man had eyes the color of the ocean, and for an instant homesickness for the Atlantic claimed her. The happiest moments of her girlhood had been stolen days at the beach, she and her mother frolicking in the surf or searching for shells, all unbeknownst to the Reverend. They were bright spots in an otherwise bleak existence.

Now, she felt certain she could gladly fall into the depths of the man's eyes. Swim there. Live there. Find freedom from the freeze that held her captive.

"Look, there's no pretty way to say this so I'm gonna lay it right out." Snow landed on the rugged plane of one cheek, but he paid it no mind. He swallowed hard. "There's some dead folks up here, lying in the snow. Keep your sights on my Stetson, you hear? Don't look down, watch my hat and follow right behind. Put a hand on the back of my jacket, so I can feel you're there. Stay with me, I'll lead you through."

He waited until she nodded.

Then he turned and stood still until she grabbed the bottom of his jacket and gave it a hard tug.

Over his shoulder, he called, "My hat—look at my hat and let me lead us."

When he strode forward she kept her gaze on the black, snow-covered Stetson and matched his pace step for step. She smelled the horror they passed, heard the screams and cries they moved beyond, and felt the heat of something burning nearby. Through it all, she kept her eyes fixed, staring at the brim of his hat.

In that moment she realized she didn't know the man's name, but she put her life and trust in him, and willingly followed him through Hell.

Chapter 5

The fastest way to get the women out of the weather wouldn't be appreciated by those of a genteel nature but conventions be damned, he had no other choice. He couldn't go for a wagon. Transporting them individually meant he'd have to leave one at the derailment until his return, and he wasn't going to do that.

Charles waited right where Tate left him, near the engine. By now, smoke no longer poured from the wreck and the man near the stack had been nearly covered by a compassionate blanket of white.

He turned to the woman who'd trailed him as closely as the tail on a puppy and searched her face for any sign she'd succumbed to shock. He couldn't blame her if that was the case. Being in a train crash didn't happen every day, so some distress seemed natural. Called for, even. But the gaze that met his showed no sign of mental lapse.

Good. If she understood what he asked, maybe she'd comply without too much fuss.

Noise around them reached a level that required he shout to be heard above the din. It looked as if most of Wylder had rushed to the scene to help. People dashed from one side of the tracks to the other, leading survivors to waiting wagons or to shelter beneath a stand of pines beyond the mess.

Others hauled satchels, broken boxes, parcels of every size and description from the cars. Some gathered what had been thrown from the train, probably through windows that smashed on impact. They placed the goods in piles.

He wondered how the freight cars fared. Were his crates intact? There hadn't been an explosion, so he figured his dynamite mightn't be damaged. He'd check later. Now, he had women to transport.

He tipped his head toward Charles' saddle. "I'm gonna get you outta here but it won't be fancy. Do you ride?"

She glanced at the large animal, her eyes rounding as her mouth fell open.

That she had eyes the palest shade of blue and sweet, bow-shaped lips didn't go unnoticed. In another time, he would've been swayed by her beauty but now his mind circled back to getting them away from here. The woman in his arms hadn't stirred one bit. She breathed, barely, so she had not gone the way of others, but that didn't mean she didn't board the Heavenly Express at this very instant.

He had to get them sheltered. Both were covered with snow and the blue-eyed blonde beauty shivered. The lips that caught his attention were tinged with blue.

"Do you ride? It's fine if you don't."

She shook her head. "That horse is too big—I can't—"

He cut her off. "No, he's perfect. He's powerful enough to carry us outta here."

She shook her head so hard hairpins flew out from the golden tresses. When she took a step back, she slipped, landing on her bottom in the snow. Her lower lip quivered, a sure sign she would not stay strong for much longer, so he crouched beside her.

"What's your name?" He forced his tone to gentle some, the way he would with a frightened animal. "I'm Tate. What's your name?"

"M-M-Margaret." Her teeth chattered. "B-but my mother called me Meg."

He smiled, holding her gaze with his own and hoping to get through to her. He already had one inert female in his arms and couldn't possibly carry another.

"That's a pretty name." He tipped his head to his mount. "Look, Charles knows the way outta here. And your friend, she needs to get inside where it's warm."

She looked at the other woman. A hand reached out to brush snow off the unconscious figure's cheek.

"O-okay."

Not as hard as he'd imagined it would be, but he hadn't gotten her on the horse yet.

"Good. Now, let's get away from here, to a warm fire and some dry clothes." When he stood a spear of pain shot through his leg. Damn, but that old war wound never did shut up. "I'm going to climb into the saddle with your friend. Then I'll reach out a hand to you. Put your foot in the stirrup and leave the rest to me."

She glanced at the strap hanging from the saddle and opened her mouth to speak but he leaned down and placed a fast kiss on her cheek. Her hand shot up to cover the spot he'd touched.

"Trust me, okay? Sealed with a kiss, I promise to get you both to safety."

He climbed onto the horse, settled the inert woman on the pommel for a second, and reached his hand out.

She hesitated, and his heart stuttered in his chest. The longer they spent in the cold, the less chance they'd have of recovering from this experience.

Finally, she took his hand and he hauled her up. They were squeezed for room, but she swung her leg over Charles' broad back, sending her skirts high. Another time he would've peeked at the leg on display, but this was no time to ogle any female—unless he wanted them dead from exposure, which he certainly did not. He circled her with his arms, cradled the other woman against her body, and grabbed the reins.

A leftward lean and quick tongue cluck turned the animal. They headed for Wylder with a snowstorm raging and the dead beginning to freeze behind them.

Tate could hardly take in the events of the last hour. Life changed in a heartbeat.

Now he simply wanted to get back to town without embarrassing himself.

The woman he'd kissed sat on his lap, closer than any female had been in longer than he cared to admit. And the thoughts running through his head? He'd believed those feelings reserved for the schoolteacher who'd saved his life all those years ago.

Traitorous body. Right when he'd declared himself a confirmed bachelor, it went and found a woman who ignited the fire he'd worked so hard to put out.

Oh, yes. She ignited a blaze within him—and managed to do so on the coldest night of the season. Damn miracle, that.

Chapter 6

Meg hoped she hadn't jumped from the frying pan straight into the fire. Riding into a snowstorm in the darkness, to who-knew-where with a man she'd barely met didn't feel like the wisest thing she'd ever done. Yet, what choice did she have?

She surely would have died in that train car had he not rescued them. The smoke invading her lungs, a second fire, or even the bone-chilling cold would have been the end of her.

Or worse. Eventually another train would come through on those tracks. The engineer had no way of knowing about the crash. When he came upon the wreck, what would stop him from slamming into the stranded cars?

Nothing.

Anything remaining on that wrecked train would be obliterated when a second train crashed into it.

Better to be in the dark with a stranger than waiting for a train to come along and send her from this world.

The man behind her pressed so intimately against her backside that keeping her mind from his anatomy and on less lively topics did test her. The thought that she entertained sinful, lustful thoughts did cross her mind—in the Reverend's voice—but she pushed it away. He had no right to enter her head anymore. She wouldn't allow it.

It brought more joy to consider the feel of her rescuer than to remember the man whom she'd fled.

She hadn't realized that being this near a man would cause reactions new to her. Every time the horse swayed a certain way, the man's...ah, well, he sent a wave of heat to her core which, given the frigid conditions, didn't feel at all unwelcome. And the way the front of his strong form pressed against her spine chased the wobbliness from her shaking body.

A short ride before lights came into view. They were muted, filtered through a screen of snow, but they were there.

Tate leaned closer and spoke beside her ear. A wave of breath warmed her cheek. "That's Wylder. My place is on this side of it."

Good. They didn't have far to go.

Her teeth chattered so hard that she didn't trust herself not to bite her own tongue, so she nodded.

The horse brought them closer and led them down what she presumed must be the main street. Buildings beyond dancing white flakes emerged. She couldn't tell what any were, but some had light falling from upper windows. Must be that shop owners lived above places, the way they did in Boston.

Boston. It felt a lifetime away. Good riddance, she thought.

The horse turned right beyond one of the biggest and fanciest buildings she'd seen so far. Light fell from every window and the faint sound of piano music met her ears. She wondered who could afford to live in a place that big.

Tate directed the horse to circle behind another building. One lamp burned in the front window as they passed. The animal walked right onto a wooden rear decking, stood beneath an overhang, and halted. It tossed its head twice, as if to say he'd completed his job.

"Look, I'm gonna lift your friend a little and put her, um, well, I'll lightly perch her on the pommel. You sneak your leg over the saddle, and when you've got both feet on the left side I'll lower you down."

The instructions weren't complicated, but her legs had gone numb, and her fingers were stiff. Her mind told her body what to do but it refused to cooperate.

"I-oh—my leg is stuck." Her skirts were frozen, having gotten wet somewhere during the incident. On the way here they'd turned to iced hard lengths of fabric, as if over-starched. She fought to move her leg from one side of the horse to the other but couldn't do it.

He reached around, leaning forward so his whole upper body pressed against her back. His hand felt beneath her skirts, landing on her calf above her boot. She wore stockings but still, no man had placed a hand on her person this way.

It did not feel bad at all. Shocking, yes. Awful? Not one bit.

"Here, let me pull you free. Your garment has you trapped and—oh, there you are." He guided her leg over the saddle, under Georgina's body, and to the point where it hung beside the other.

The ground looked miles away.

Fear made her do something she'd never done before: Meg pressed herself against Tate, wrapped her arms around his broad shoulders, and hid her face against his neck. The scent of smoke, sweat, and something spicy swept up her nostrils.

A tear slid from the corner of one eye, making her shiver at its hot touch against her frozen cheek.

"Hey, we're home. No need to be frightened." He tucked a fingertip beneath her chin and lifted it. She met his gaze and saw comfort in the deep blue depths. "Trust me. Hold my hand, I'll swing you down."

She took a deep breath and put her hand in his. The fingers that held her were work-worn and calloused, their grip secure enough that his hand felt like an extension of her own. Before she could say a word, he lifted her clear of the saddle and swung her over the side of the horse. Her toes touched ground and she stepped back.

Tate pulled Georgina close, raised a leg over the saddle, and slid down.

"Come on, let's get you two out of the night air."

She followed him to the back door, then inside. They walked through a dark room toward the light she'd seen from the street. A fire burned in the hearth here, but he didn't stop.

They dropped snow on the floorboards, but it didn't appear to bother him. The front room held little: crates, some shelving, and a bedroll. A long counter ran the back length of the room. Behind it, a door.

He nodded. "This way."

Beyond the door, a small room with a staircase. The man took the stairs two at a time, and although she noticed he limped he carried his cargo as if she weighed less than a sack filled with feathers.

At the top of the stairs, a landing. A window, a hallway, and two open doors. He headed into the room at the right, which, if she guessed correctly, sat directly above the large downstairs room.

A fire burned in the hearth. The furnishings surprised her with their elegance. The Reverend's home lacked what he called "ostentation" in favor of hard, straight lines and cushion-less chairs. She'd grown up in a box with unyielding floors to punish knees of sinners and no softness at all that would, in his opinion, encourage impure thoughts.

This room looked like sinner's paradise. The bedstead's carved posts, matching wardrobes, and side tables, all crafted with a deep red wood finish, intrigued her. Even in her chilled state, she appreciated their beauty.

Toward the front of the room, before a wide window, white cloths draped shapes that she guessed were a chaise, side chairs, and settee. She'd heard about bed chambers large enough to accommodate sitting rooms but had never seen one.

Fancy stopped short of the utilitarian bedding. Two pillows, a true luxury, propped against the headboard. The wool blankets and blue muslin sheets were serviceable but not elaborate like the rest of the room.

Tate placed his burden down with gentleness that impressed her. The man didn't know them at all, yet here he stood, offering shelter in his home and, if she had it right, his own bed.

He rubbed his hands together to warm them. Then he leaned down and lifted first one of Georgina's eyelids, then the other. He straightened and furrowed his brow.

His expression scared her.

"Is she okay? Do we need a doctor?"

He met her gaze. "It wouldn't hurt to have Doc

look at her, but I bet he's got his hands full with all the injuries from the train. Lots of folks were bleeding and I saw some with what looked like broken bits so tracking him down to take a gander at an unconscious woman might not be a good idea."

She saw his point. Still, she didn't want to lose her new—and only—friend.

"What can I do to help her?"

He crossed the room and pulled open the wide door to a huge wardrobe. Motioning her over, he held his arms out to the contents of the piece. She blinked at the sheer number of dresses, blouses, skirts, and frilly women's clothing hanging from hooks and a wooden rod. To one side, horizontal rows of shelves, filled with folded clothing, stole her breath.

She'd never seen so many pretty things in one place.

"There are towels in that." He pointed to a chest of drawers in one corner. "Use whatever you want. And dress warmly, to chase the chill away." He hesitated. "Do you think you can remove her clothing and dress her on your own, or do you need a hand?"

Meg looked back to where her friend lay. His offer to help seemed sincere but they'd experienced too many indignities already for one day. She could not allow a stranger to see either of them in an indelicate state. Exhaustion threatened to claim her, and her arms and legs wobbled a bit, but she mustered the strength to shake her head.

"No help needed, thank you. I can take care of her."

He nodded. "Holler if you change your mind."

Tate went to the door and walked into the hallway.

"Tate?"

He stuck his head back into the room. "Yes?"

"Thank you for rescuing us."

Chapter 7

"Good work, Charles." He'd brushed and fed the horse. Now he laid a blanket over his back and rubbed the sweet spot above his nose one last time. The animal leaned into the touch and a wave of gratitude swept over Tate.

Without Charles, he'd still be on foot somewhere in the center of this country. He'd made it this far because of the devoted animal's service. They were like family, he and the horse.

The two wagon horses had been cared for, as well. Now they stood in their stalls, bedded down for the night.

He headed for the open door and stood there, looking out at the storm. Snow still fell in swirling waves that shook trees and dumped accumulations onto the ground. He'd shoveled out the wagon before pulling it inside the barn. He had no idea how much snow had fallen, only that it brought turmoil to Wylder, and just over a week before Christmas, at that.

He sucked in a deep breath.

Christmas. The last time he'd been here, Violet had been in charge of the holiday party for the town. He figured that as Wylder's schoolteacher the responsibility for putting it on still fell on her shoulders. How he would feel when he saw her again, he couldn't tell.

But he didn't need to know now. He pulled the barn door closed behind him and headed for the building. That the place belonged to him still hit him like a pail of cold water, shocked him right from his head to his toes.

Inside, he hurried out of his wet garments and hung them to dry before the fire after he pulled on some dry things. He considered going back with the wagon and collecting some scattered belongings but that could wait for morning. Now, he had two survivors to care for.

He lit a fire in the cookstove and set the kettle on. It came as a great help that so many household items came with the purchase. He'd never be this well outfitted otherwise.

Footsteps on the stairs alerted him to the woman's presence. The kitchen area, tucked in the corner of the back room, had its own door that led to the staircase, so he opened it. She stood a few steps from the bottom, a lamp in her hand.

"I hope you don't mind my coming down." She had changed into a light blue dress that matched the color of her eyes. A dark blue shawl wrapped around her shoulders, held together with her free hand, gave the impression that she entertained late-night kitchen chats often.

"I'm glad you did. I thought to bring a tray up to you and..." He had a woman under his roof whose identity he did not know. He didn't realize that fact until this very minute.

"Georgina. That is very kind of you, but you've already done so much for us."

He stepped back so she could pass through the doorway. When she entered the kitchen, he closed the door to keep down the draft from the staircase.

"I haven't done anything anyone else wouldn't do." He scraped a hand through his hair. Still damp, but drying thanks to warm air produced by the fires in the hearths. "You must be hungry."

She glanced down at her feet, clad in a pair of soft slippers, then raised her gaze to meet his. A small shrug, and an admission. "I wouldn't refuse a bite."

As if on cue, his stomach rumbled. The noise in the otherwise-quiet room caught them both off guard. She raised an eyebrow and tried to hide her amusement.

He grinned and rubbed a hand over his belly. "I guess we both could use some food."

She moved closer. He'd laid eggs, bread, a pitcher of milk, and a small chunk of cheese he'd brought from California.

"May I?"

Turning down a woman who wanted to cook for him? Not going to happen. His southern mother had raised a polite son, not a stupid one.

"Thank you." He pointed to the pots hanging near the stove and a drawer filled with kitchen odds and ends. "I think you'll find what you need in this mess. I haven't looked through it all—heck, I don't have any idea what half of it is, but I have a feeling you do."

She shot him a shy smile. "Why don't you go sit? This will only take a few minutes."

He didn't argue. The leg throbbed like a piece of meat pummeled by an angry housewife. He pulled out a chair at the table and sat. Getting off it brought a sigh, one that didn't go unnoticed.

A glance his way. Her brows were furrowed. "Are you okay? You didn't hurt yourself out at the wreck, did you?"

She stirred eggs in a blue earthenware bowl with the confidence of someone who knew her way about a kitchen. He'd watched her crack those eggs one-handed, something he'd seen a weathered old cook on the trail do once but never anyone else.

How she prepared a meal and watched him at the same time, he didn't know.

"Nah, no worries about the train." He ran a hand down his thigh to his knee, then back up again. The spot where he'd been shot still tingled when he touched it, all these years later. "It's an old war wound, a reminder that I'm mortal."

She poured the eggs into a cast iron skillet. He waited to see if she'd stir them right away, but she didn't. He liked a woman wise enough to be patient.

"We all need that, don't we? A reminder that life can be cut off in a heartbeat and—oh…" The wooden spoon slid into the pan when she put a hand over her mouth. A tear slipped down her cheek, so Tate stood and went to stand behind her.

His arm went around her shoulders and the woman leaned back against him without a fuss. Her body trembled, and he felt fear. He'd been a fool to think she'd get over the derailment so quickly. She'd nearly been killed, and her friend lay upstairs at this very moment. Who could tell what weighed on Meg's heart and mind? Damn, but he'd been selfish to let her cook after her harrowing experience.

Tate grabbed a towel, wrapped it around the hot handle, and moved the heavy skillet off the burner. He turned her around to face him and pulled her against his chest. The tears came then, a flood as fast and furious as a tidal surge. When she stopped sobbing he held her while she sniffled and hiccupped.

She'd brushed her hair, leaving it to hang loose down her back, so he stroked the silky waves. They were the color of Kansas wheat, gold and glowing. He hadn't thought about those wheat fields in a long time. Now the memory brought a smile and a tug on his heart.

Her head came away from his chest. She raised her gaze to his with a shy shoulder shrug. "I'm sorry. I don't know what came over me."

He brought a fingertip to touch the tear hanging on the end of one long eyelash and wiped it away. "You don't have anything to apologize for. What happened to you is going to take time to get over. I shouldn't have you cooking for us. Why don't you sit down, and I'll finish up here?"

Her gaze didn't leave his when she shook her head. "No. I can't do that."

He felt himself falling under the spell of her pale blue eyes. After the tears they sparkled like jewels and he couldn't pull his gaze away. "Why not?"

"I need to show my appreciation." She dropped her voice to a whisper. "You saved my life."

His throat tightened. "Maybe. But you don't owe me a thing."

The pink tip of her tongue as it swept delicately across her lower lip about did him in. It had been so long since he'd held a woman this close. Blood raced through his veins like a runaway stallion and when she hitched a breath he nearly crushed her against him.

"I owe you so much that I haven't been able to think of anything else." She hesitated, then whispered,

"You kissed me."

Something low in his gut tightened. Heat spread in a wave out from his center, drying his mouth. For a moment, he couldn't speak. "I did."

Meg colored, the pink rising on her cheeks so alluring that his heart skipped a beat. She looked into his eyes and murmured, "I didn't mind it one bit."

Chapter 8

Meg had never sat across a table from a kind or handsome man. Truth be told, the only man she'd shared meals with, the Reverend, could not be called good-looking or even-tempered, so this came as a treat.

They'd finished cooking together, another first experience for her but one she enjoyed greatly. Tate saved the eggs from being tough and she toasted thick slices of bread. The pantry offerings were basic, but she found a pot of raspberry jam that brought sweetness to their humble fare.

Coffee, strong and black, rounded out the meal. They ate without hurrying, as if it were a decent dinner hour instead of well past nightfall. As they sat, she heard the sound of wagons rumbling past.

"Do you think that more people from the train are coming to town?" She wondered what lay beyond Tate's residence. The darkness kept her from knowing but she thought that maybe more homes were past his. "Families down the street, taking folks in, the way you did for me and Georgina?"

A look passed over his face, one she could not fathom. He avoided her gaze but straightened his features before he nodded. "I'm sure the wagons are filled with folks from the train." He took a bite of toast and chewed. After swallowing, he added, "Wylder is a hospitable place. Your traveling companions will be looked after."

She stuck her fork into a piece of egg but didn't bring it to her mouth. "I traveled alone. No companions for me, I'm afraid."

"If I may be so bold, where are you headed?"

A logical question but she had no reasonable reply. Where? Anywhere far enough away from the Reverend to feel safe. She couldn't say that, although it happened to be the truth.

She put the eggs in her mouth and chewed, buying a bit of time. "I didn't have a destination, actually. I thought I'd see a place and decide to stop for a while but so far I haven't found anywhere to linger. I do have to say, though, that Chicago seemed interesting but then I met Georgina and she planned to travel to Laramie. How could I stay in Chicago when my only friend prepared to board a train?"

She realized her mouth ran away from her, so she snapped her lips closed. Raising her eyes to see how he took her revelations, she crossed her fingers beneath the table and hoped he'd been like the Reverend, too busy eating to bother listening to what came from her mouth.

No such luck. The man across from her placed his fork on the edge of his plate and folded his hands on the table. His gaze, so serious and concerned, made her gut clench. She'd spoken out of turn. Surely he would reproach her for being so foolish. He might even tell someone that she traveled alone—the railroad, maybe. There had been no sign indicating that they prohibited women from riding their trains unaccompanied, but one could never tell.

If she were able to smack herself for her stupidity she would have done so.

"You're traveling on your own? No friend or family member to accompany you?"

She tossed her hair with what she hoped came across as casual indifference. "That's right." Pointing with the top end of her fork to his plate, she said, "You should eat while they're hot. No one likes cold eggs, do they?"

She did not sidetrack him by referring to his meal. Mother said that men thought with what sat below their belts so she expected his stomach would take precedence over her actions.

"Is someone waiting for your arrival?" He scrubbed a hand across his chin. The sound of whiskers rasping against his palm sent a shiver up her spine. What an interesting noise! "Wait, I'm not thinking clearly. You said you don't have a set destination, so you don't have anyone looking to meet your train."

Mother had been wrong. This man did not think with his below-the-belt stomach, but with his head. He'd puzzled out her story in less time than it took to eat an egg.

She couldn't be sure, but she thought he might be the most intelligent man she'd ever met.

And that included the Reverend, who could recite every line of the Good Book without looking at a page.

"That's right. I'm traveling alone, with no destination in mind. There isn't any law against that, is there?" She added a note of challenge to her voice to let him see she wasn't without a mind of her own.

"No, of course there isn't. I'm surprised, is all." He picked up his fork and poked the food on his plate around a bit. She watched him, and saw he searched for what to say. He pushed at his eggs. When he met her gaze, he lifted his shoulders, then let them fall. She noticed the way his shirt pulled tight when he moved. "I would think that a woman like you, with such charm, would have someone waiting on you. That's what I'm trying to say."

It had been a long day, a disastrous one at that, but the man pulled happiness from her tired soul. Meg softened her tone. "No one waiting on me, I'm afraid. No one to care where I am or what I do." She took a deep breath. "Makes life kind of simple, really. I come and go as I please without explanations."

They resumed eating. The silence stretched but it did not bring discomfort. She'd been wary her entire life, never knowing when to expect a hard exchange. Being prepared for the worst didn't give her much quiet time. But now, things were different, and she leaned into this pocket of peace.

Tate finished first. He sat back in his chair and watched the fire burn in the hearth. She liked that he didn't rush her or make her feel like a bug on a fingertip, something to be flicked aside. He let her be.

When she put her fork down on the empty plate, he tipped his chin toward his chest. "Feel better?"

"I do. Thank you for the meal."

"You're the one who cooked. I should be thanking you."

"I believe we both prepared this meal, remember?"

A nod. "Seems you're right about that." He waited a bit before he went on. "Tomorrow at sunup I'm going back to the derailment, to see if I can help clear the mess. I'll take the wagon and bring back whatever got scattered in the wreck. I expect there'll be a central area in town where folks can go collect their belongings."

She felt she should offer to go with him, but her tummy turned upside down at the thought of returning to the crash site. Her hands grew clammy, and her mouth went dry, but she took a deep breath and prepared herself.

He spoke before she could open her mouth.

"No need for you to go back there. I know you'll want to, but I think it would be better if you stay here with your friend. She's gonna need you when she wakes up." He nodded as if the matter had been settled.

Gratitude swept through her. "If you think that's best."

"I do."

Chapter 9

Snow spiraled past Tate's face, making it nearly impossible to see between damage to the terrain and the horror brought with the accident. The derailment appeared worse now than it had in the heat of the moment, a horror his mind struggled to witness.

Train cars lay scattered in the snow like toys tossed aside after a giant's play. Deep, dark grooves in the earth, piles of frozen dirt and yellowed scrub at their sides, as if enormous fingertips gouged trails. Pines and aspens, snapped to bits, discarded embellishments to the garish scene.

But no angry goliath created this spectacle. No temper tantrum to cause a disaster of this magnitude.

Snow obscured the worst bits and turned fires to smoldering piles that sent trails of gray and black smoke into the air. Strange to see smoke rising from the same spot where snow piled high. He didn't think he'd ever witnessed such a thing before—and he hoped to never again.

Tate slowed the horses, mindful of the carnage. He didn't know if bodies were all recovered or if some still rested beneath the snow.

Several inches had fallen overnight but it could not soften the scene. He guided the horses to follow the steps and wheel tracks already in place. If others made it through without a misstep, he should, too.

A man rode toward him. The way he sat astride his horse seemed familiar, but the snow fell in a dense sheet that made it impossible to tell for sure whether they'd met two years ago, or not.

He kept moving, hoping the bumps beneath the wagon wheels were not bodies. After walking around his brothers in arms where they lay dying on battlefields during the war, he had no stomach for dishonoring the dead now.

Had he not been concerned with the freight cars he might've stayed in Wylder, back in the nice, warm building he still couldn't believe belonged to him. He had the paperwork to prove it but, damn, it seemed like a dream.

And this, the continuation of a nightmare.

The rider pulled up beside him.

Tate touched the brim of his hat, sending snow falling past his nose. "Sheriff."

Earl Hanson shook his head, tipping his chin toward his jacket and slapping his lapel.

He wore what looked to be the same worn, brown hat he'd had the last time they'd seen each other. "No badge here. I ain't the sheriff any longer, but I'm glad to find out I made an impression on you. It's been, what, two, maybe three years since you left town?"

Wind swept snow into his face, so he tucked his chin and waited a spell, a couple of long moments before it died down enough to reply. The ex-lawman sat with a stoicism rarely seen outside of carved statues, the kind on display in fancy southern graveyards. With so much death and destruction surrounding them it came as no stretch to picture him that way.

"Good memory. Two years." He swept a hand over

his face, wishing the damn snow would lighten up or at least stop stinging his eyes like tiny frozen needles. "Rode out Christmas day."

"Come back to see Miss Bloom, have you?"

Once a lawman, always a lawman, he thought. Bile rose in his throat. How would he keep this guy off his tail or from uncovering what should stay buried?

"Nossir, not this time." Waving an arm toward the tracks, he changed the subject, hoping to throw attention elsewhere. "How's it looking down the line? The freight cars damaged or are they on the rails?"

The man looked back. With limited visibility, he had to be remembering what he'd seen. Tate watched as the other man wrangled with his reply.

"A mix of both. I've seen a lot in my days but I ain't never seen a mess like this." He nodded to the wagon. "Hoping to pick up something you been waitin' on?"

Enough. Speaking with the retired sheriff felt like an interrogation so Tate snapped the reins and set the wagon horses in motion. He nodded as he pulled away. "I am. Nice seein' you, Hanson."

"Same, Taylor."

So the old man remembered his name. Apprehension shot through him. It did not bode well that he did. Not well at all.

The farther they moved into the disaster scene, the more handling the horses required. They stepped gingerly thorough the destruction and needed coaxing to move past the engine car. Someone removed the body from the smokestack. He wondered who had the grisly duty of taking the engineer from his final assignment.

The sight of the overturned car where he'd rescued the two women made his stomach roll. A miracle that anyone survived being in there. Soot colored the front side. Window coverings hung in scorched shreds like hellacious icicles.

He wondered where the child he'd seen ended up. He hoped its mother had been found. Life dumped misery on the undeserving—and that little one surely didn't deserve any part in this.

His attention wandered for barely an instant, but it proved to be a crucial one.

Two draft horses pulled the wagon. He had no attachment to either and hadn't named them after their purchase a few days back. They were work animals, that's all. But they were necessary, so when the left-hand one stumbled he leaned back on the reins. The other shimmied sideways, tugging to pull the connecting pole into place.

One horse went down so fast the huge beast lay in the snow in a heartbeat.

Tate jumped to the ground and ran to the where the horse writhed. Keeping clear of thrashing hooves, he made his way to the animal's head but could not get close.

A grimy part of the train's undercarriage, uncovered by the horse's hooves, stuck up out of the snow. Blood splattered around it, evidence that the animal had stepped on the concealed debris.

The downed horse attracted attention. Its squeals cut the air, sending chills up his spine.

A man rode over, dismounted, and hurried to stand beside him. Tate looked up and saw, through the snow falling in sheets between them, a man he could've lived all the days of his life without ever seeing again.

If he didn't have bad luck he'd have no luck at all. His brother, lost at Gettysburg, used to say it and neither doubted it might have been on the family crest centuries ago.

Thomas Harvey, the man who claimed his beloved Violet's heart, clapped a hand on his shoulder. A surge rose within him and instead of being grateful for the other's presence, he leaned away from his touch.

"Damn bad luck, Tate." Harvey squatted, then pointed to a foreleg. "For a minute I thought I saw snow but that white sticking out is bone."

He leaned in to examine the horse while the other man held its head still. A couple of other guys, men he didn't know, stopped to assist. Upon closer inspection, they saw the bone had not broken cleanly. There were protrusions from more than one point on the leg, and when he ran a hand over the snow to clean the blood away, he felt grit. Fragments, most likely.

And just like that, he lost a horse. No way an animal could recover from something like this.

They worked together to unhitch the poor thing. When the remaining horse and wagon were free, one of the men moved it beyond the scene.

Tate hated killing anything, man or beast. He'd done too much during the war to ever feel his conscience at ease. He figured he'd sent souls to Heaven, but would probably never get his own past the Pearly Gates. He hoped for leniency for soldiers, and in this moment prayed it spread to cover mercy killings.

Harvey's horse had been moved, too. They remained with the animal and now he hollered over the howling wind. "I'll help you drag the carcass over there. Some of the others will, too. We can leave it under those trees, out of the way. Don't want anyone falling over it and it makes it hard to get wagons past." He kicked the metal that caused the fall. "A couple of us should move this. Losing one horse is bad enough. We don't need another to go down."

Tate dropped his head back and let snow fall on his face for an instant. Then, he lowered his gaze to the pitiful creature lying on the ground in a circle of blood and snow and reached for his holster.

Chapter 10

Tate brought the wagon up sharp at the bottom of the steps in front of the Five Star Saloon. He jumped from the bench seat onto the ground where his boots slid on the slick snow, and he came close to falling on his behind. His nerves frayed, he grabbed the side of the wagon to steady himself, then set out for the door.

He stopped long enough to brush the worst of the snow accumulation off his shoulders. Grabbing his hat from his head, he slapped it against his palm and pushed inside. The batwing doors opened with a groan, as if they, too, knew of the town's disaster.

The saloon didn't see this many bodies on a summer's Saturday night after ranch hands and cattle drivers received their pay and went looking for a good time. The crush of folks spilled into every corner, but this wasn't the Five Star's typical crowd.

He nodded to an elderly couple seated at a table inside the doorway. The woman looked chilled and had a faded red lap blanket across her legs.

A young woman held the hands of two little girls dressed in matching traveling coats. Their eyes were huge and when they looked up at him, he winked. One covered her mouth with her free hand and giggled. The other winked back.

He pressed through the throng, headed toward the bar. Snippets of conversation met his ears, giving him a picture of what happened that gave meaning to the bits and pieces he'd brought back in the wagon. These were real people, with lives. They were more than an unfortunate accident, more than a headline for the weekly *Wylder Sun*.

"I had a ham sandwich in my hand. I have no idea where it ended up…"

"My mother gave me a book to read but when it grew dark I closed my eyes. The next thing I knew, the train went airborne!"

"Ellen didn't make it…she hit her head hard…I'll hear her scream for as long as I live, I swear I will…"

"I hear they've got bodies piled high at the undertaker's place. Doubtful he's got enough pine boxes for all of those folks."

"We both got out without any trouble. Slipped in the snow, tore the knee outta my good traveling trousers, but it's a small price to pay for our lives."

Sorrow mixed with relief, so tangible Tate could taste it. He kept his gaze on the bottles behind the bar. It took too much strength to look these folks in the eyes, to take on their emotions. Better to focus on something that would let him take a step back, for a few minutes, from this horror.

He bellied up to the bar. Most of the glasses on its top weren't beer mugs or shot glasses, but coffee mugs. A few empty plates scattered about solidified the idea that folks were taking their morning meals here.

The man behind the bar wasn't familiar. Tate waved him over but shook his head when the barkeep held up a tin coffee pot. With a haggard expression and bloodshot eyes, it looked like he needed the coffee more than anyone else did.

"Whiskey. Two fingers."

The man put the pot down, grabbed a shot glass and a bottle, and poured. He placed it in front of Tate and asked, "Been out to the site?"

He raised the glass to his lips and tipped his head back. The booze went down smooth, leaving a trail of heat in its wake. Nice to get that warmth. He needed it. His whole body had gone colder than a penguin's pecker.

"I have." He put the glass down. "Again."

The man poured. "What's it looks like out there? Can't really tell from listening to people. Everyone's got a different story, dependin' on where they were sittin'."

He downed the shot. More heat, enough this time for a satisfying sigh after he swallowed. Dropping the glass to the bar, he ran a hand across his face. When he removed it, the bartender hadn't moved and stared at him as if he expected to learn one of the great mysteries of life.

"Ever imagine what hell looks like?"

A nod. Then he poured a third shot.

"Well, it's like this. Take that hell in your mind and pretend it's a woman gettin' ready for a picnic. A fancy one, where she'll dress up to impress, to make herself as spectacular as possible." He paused long enough to down the alcohol and place the shot glass back on the bar.

"I had me a woman like that once. Fancy." The man filled the glass.

Tate warmed to the subject now that all that whiskey flowed in him.

"Imagine the train is the woman. A woman throws

on a hat, gloves, earbobs, maybe a spritz of something smellin' like gardenias or roses and does her hair up real nice. Get what I'm sayin'?"

The other man nodded. "I do."

Tate warmed to the conversation. He waved his left hand in the air, seeing the wreck in his mind as he pointed it out for the man behind the bar.

"The train? It leaves the tracks, turns cars on their sides, has fires break out so things get nice and charred, tosses belongings into the snow, slices trees off right at ground level, throws people—dead and alive, mind you—out windows into snowbanks. Then, for fun, it cooks up a couple of folks, so everyone catches a whiff of burned flesh."

He picked up the glass and eyed it. When he walked in he hadn't intended to drink this much but he could not get the stench of bodies, blood, and fried flesh out of his head. Whiskey didn't remove anything, but at least when alcoholically dulled he could pretend it didn't exist.

Damn, but this felt too much like the war for comfort.

He stared into the other man's rounded eyes. "You ever smell a man burning? Cooking in his own juices, his flesh seared so hot it's falling from his bones?"

The man shook his head. His mouth hung open, showing he missed a number of teeth. "Can't say I have."

The whiskey slid down and this time when he put the glass on the bar, he turned it over. He met the bartender's gaze and asked, "Who's in charge of the passengers' luggage? I've got a wagonful outside. I want to get it unloaded so I can go back to the train and get more."

The man seemed glad for the subject change. He raised a shaky arm and pointed toward the street.

"Around the side, not down Sidewinder Lane but toward the back street. I think they're pilin' things under the overhang at the church. Maybe in the church, even. Priest's not too happy about it but he'll get used to the idea."

He dropped cash on the bar and raised his hand. "Appreciate it."

Exiting seemed less arduous than coming inside the establishment had. And that stayed true to life. He didn't remember many nights when he didn't feel looser leaving a saloon than entering.

The horse waited with a resigned air, almost as if she knew she'd been spared her partner's fate. It might've been the booze, but he thought she gave him a grateful nod.

He climbed into the seat, turned the wagon toward the back of the saloon, and wished he didn't have to return to the site. No one had an exact count yet, but enough lives were lost that the place spooked him a bit.

The undertaker, Gus Wright, must be grateful for the business. Probably busier than anyone in Wylder banging out coffins for all the victims.

Tate sucked in a deep breath. Hell, maybe now that he had some whiskey under his belt he'd be less jittery. He sure hoped so because he hadn't yet been able to claim his explosives. So far, no one knew what he waited on and he aimed to keep it that way.

Nitroglycerine could be unstable, and he didn't want to be the one who blew the town to kingdom come. And if it blew, he didn't want everyone to know he'd done it.

He had to find his freight—and fast, before someone else did.

Chapter 11

Circling past the Wylder School on his way back to the train happened to be a mistake. A big one. It wasn't as if he were unfamiliar with who rang the schoolmistress' bell. He'd been avoiding the place for weeks.

The booze fuzzed up his head enough for him to forget to be cautious.

His brother's voice rang in his mind, reminding him of his bad luck, when he saw Violet standing by the wishing well in front of the schoolhouse. Her gaze lifted when he came into view and her mouth opened in surprise.

The devil sat on his shoulder, urging him to drive on by, but he couldn't do it. Not even with so much whiskey in his gut, he didn't have the wherewithal to blow past.

His mother had raised her sons to be respectful—even when intoxicated.

He slowed the horse. When the wagon stopped, he jumped down.

"Tate Taylor, as I live and breathe. Why, I didn't know you're back in Wylder." She held her coat closed beneath her chin. She should've worn gloves in this weather, but he was glad she didn't. Without them he saw her truth. No wedding ring on her finger, although he knew she and Harvey were still keeping company.

"What are you doing here?"

"What are you doing out in this weather?" He offered his arm to her. She placed a hand on his forearm, so he leaned close and asked, "Where are you headed?"

Her brow furrowed. She brought her nose high and sniffed. "Is that alcohol I smell on your breath?"

He shouldn't have stopped. Hard enough that he had snow down his back, icy feet, and missing explosives. Now the only woman he'd ever loved stood looking at him like he'd been swimming in the stuff instead of fortifying himself to go back to a grisly scene.

"Let me take you to where you're going. You could fall out here and freeze to death." He took a step, but she remained in place, so he turned to her. "Violet, please. Let's get you back to the schoolhouse."

His heart dropped when she pulled her hand off his arm and pointed a very schoolteacher-ish finger at him. "I do not need you to get me anywhere, Mister Taylor. If you'll excuse me, I've got people to see."

"Violet, please..."

"That's Miss Bloom to you, sir."

The cold shoulder felt more like a frigid, heart-numbing shoulder when she delivered it. He searched for something to say to smooth things over, but his mind went blank.

Maybe it froze, he thought.

She did not meet his gaze but did not look down, either, as she tried to walk past him. Snow fell fast and hard, as if all the angels in heaven hurled it down onto them. Visibility and sure footing were non-existent.

Her boot slipped.

A leg slid.

Arms windmilled.

When he reached for her, she shoved him aside.

And that's how Miss Violet Bloom, Wylder's schoolteacher, landed in a tangle of skirts and snow at his feet. Tate stared down at her for an instant and wondered if his luck had taken a new turn.

Then he knelt and offered her his hand.

"Get away from me!" She swatted at him as if he were a mosquito buzzing around her head. "I don't need your help."

"I'm no teacher but it sure looks like you could use a hand." Kneeling in snow during a storm had to be one of the dumbest things for an adult to do. The fabric covering his knee grew wet, one more spot on his body primed for freezing. "C'mon, let's get you up so we can both get in out of the weather."

She kicked at the tangle of skirts wrapped around her legs. He'd never seen her irate. He didn't dare tell her, especially not when she looked angrier than a wet hen, but it amused him to see her so discombobulated.

"Leave me alone, Tate."

"Why are you so fired up mad at me?"

She shot him a hard look. Even with snow covering her cheeks and lying on her back like an overturned turtle beside a stone wishing well, she turned a man's head.

"Why are you liquored up? And so early in the day, no less?"

The words refused to form in his mouth. He couldn't tell her of the stench of burnt flesh or the heaviness in his chest when he recalled the agonized look in the eyes of the horse he'd lost. His lips remained closed while he stared down at her.

He'd fallen in love with Violet when she saved his life in a makeshift hospital in Charleston. He'd been shot on the battlefield and bled so profusely he believed he wouldn't live to see another day. But this angel of mercy happened upon him and saved his undeserving soul. She'd done it with a smile and kind word, too. He'd learned two years back, when he made his way to Wylder to see her again, that she thought he would die then. His living shocked them both.

He swallowed around the lump in his throat. He owed the lady his life. That he hesitated to pick her up out of the snow showed a lack of character.

"Come on." His hand went out to her, but she scowled at it. "I've got to get back to the train. Let me do right by you and get you inside. Please."

With a sigh, she put her hand in his. They were both cold, gloveless and nearing frostbite. They clasped each other securely. That her touch did not send a river of excitement along his veins to explode in his heart, the way it always had before, crossed his mind. Strange, this shift from instant explosion to…nothing.

He'd learned that life changes in a heartbeat, even when his heart beat over a bellyful of booze in the street during a raging snowstorm. And contemplating why it didn't race at her touch would have to wait for another time.

Now, he had to get the lady out of the snow— without unnecessary thinking.

He leaned over, tightened his grip even more, and prepared to tug her up.

The same instant, Violet threw her energy into extricating herself. She yanked on his arm with so much force that he fell on top of her.

"Oof!" Tate stared at the woman whose face suddenly appeared inches from his own.

"Oh!" Her eyes rounded but she didn't try to push him off.

"Violet, I—"

"Tate, I'm sorry, I—"

"I should—"

"Yes, you should—"

He put a hand down beside her head. Maybe the liquor affected him or perhaps his senses had flown off on their own, but he didn't feel the snow beneath his palm. His heart hammered in his chest and the nearness of her sent his mind spiraling as senselessly as the snowflakes twirling in the air around them.

Her violet-hued eyes were as lovely as he'd recalled. They appeared often in his dreams but his imagination didn't do them justice. Big, beautiful, and so clear they sparkled, they made him feel as if he could see into her soul.

Or at least, that's how he'd felt before. Now, they were pretty, and her face as comely as ever. Her figure fit beneath his form exactly as he'd imagined it would.

It hit him hard. The fire had gone out. His mind spun—how could he not feel completely beside himself, finally being this close to her? He'd dreamed of this moment almost his whole life—yet now a new realization, this emptiness, chased out every other feeling.

Tate closed the gap between their faces.

He touched her lips with his own. They were cold, but soft. And when he moved his mouth against hers, she responded. No big heat, but a tender kiss.

A good-bye kiss.

He pulled away and they stared at each other. He saw confusion mirrored in the wide-eyed look she gave him. A pang of regret shot to his heart, but it came too late. He couldn't undo what had already been done, as much as he wished it were possible.

Snow fell on her cheeks. He brushed a gentle thumb over the flakes.

A thread of sadness wound around his soul at the recognition the flame he'd carried for this beautiful woman had gone out. She would always be his personal angel on earth, but only in his mind—and never his arms.

He gazed into her eyes and saw the truth. They were not meant to be together. The mood swept over him without sorrow. He simply didn't feel for her the way he'd believed he did. Something had changed— and it was not due to the whiskey.

There were no words, so he didn't offer any.

He placed both hands in the snow beside her head and lifted his body off hers. He reached a hand to her. When she placed hers in his, he yanked her to her feet and took a step back, giving her room to pass.

Violet brushed by without looking at him. It seemed she, too, had run out of things to say.

Chapter 12

Tate piled the last crate in the far corner of the barn. They'd need to be moved, but for now, the shelter offered a dry spot that would have to do until he figured out a better situation.

He'd worked all day, bringing personal belongings from the train to town.

Then he'd helped empty the freight cars. A dozen wagons transported cargo to various locations. Empty storage space during the winter proved difficult to find. Families stocked up to sustain their own until the spring thaw, but they'd managed to tuck everything they salvaged away. And men who waited on deliveries, the way he did, claimed their goods.

His body ached. The old wound fairly screamed as he closed the barn door and headed for the building. He'd yet to think of it as a house or home, even. The living space above the storefront made it his home but since he'd never envisioned himself living like a shopkeeper, the place didn't feel snug.

Maybe time would change that. Now, all he wanted could be found in the big tin bathtub. Hot water, lots of it, and a good, long time to soak his battered body.

Maybe a shot or two out of that whiskey bottle tucked in the cupboard. For medicinal purposes, of course.

He leaned a shoulder against the back door and

pushed it open. The wind had cut down some, but the weather still made ordinary chores challenging. Everything required extra effort and he'd nearly come to the end of his reserves.

The aroma that met him as he stepped over the threshold brought liquid to his mouth. Whatever sat on the cookstove smelled divine. He sniffed. Potatoes, carrots, beans, if he guessed right. He inhaled again. Apples and cinnamon, too.

"Welcome home." Meg crossed the room. Dressed in another blue dress with an apron over the skirt, and her hair done up, she didn't look at all like someone who'd been pulled from a crash. She held her hand out. "Here, let me take your wet jacket and hat. I'll put them near the fire to dry."

It took a minute for it to get into his head that this beautiful woman wanted to wait on him. When it did, he fumbled with the buttons on his coat. A thin skim of ice covered the wooden rounds, and his chilled fingertips could not unfasten them.

"Here, let me help."

She came so close the scent of lavender swept up his nose. Her golden head dipped as she focused on his jacket front. The sweetest thing any woman had done for him, unbuttoning his garment with dedicated concentration.

His body might be cold and weary, but he hadn't died yet. Heat flooded his core and swept down, low enough to bring part of his anatomy to near attention.

Tate cleared his throat to take his mind from where it threatened to roam.

When the buttons were open, she pushed the heavy fabric off his shoulders and pulled it from his arms.

Sarita Leone

Then she stood, with his jacket in one hand, and held the other hand out. "Your hat?"

He took it from his head and handed it over. Suddenly conscious of how he looked, he ran a hand through the mess that had been hidden by the Stetson.

"Thanks for the help. I must look a sight." He ran his hand over his chin. There had been no time—or need—to shave before he left this morning. Now whiskers grated his palm. "I'm sorry. You look so pretty, and here I am, wet and dirty, dripping in your kitchen."

She placed the garments near the fire, then turned to face him. "Your kitchen." Her smile made the room seem as bright as a meadow on a spring day.

The only sound in the place, the fires crackling in hearths and the cookstove. He tilted his head, listening for the sign of another moving around anywhere beneath this roof but silence greeted him.

"Your friend? How is she doing?"

God, he hoped she hadn't died while he had been away!

A smile relieved him of the breath he held.

"Georgina is awake. Well, not at this moment, she's gone back to sleep, but she woke earlier and is doing well." Meg pulled her lower lip between her teeth as her gaze dropped to the floor.

Something made her uncomfortable. "Are you sure she's okay? Do you need me to fetch Doc? I don't mind—I can track him down. Heard he's spending a lot of time at the saloon."

She raised her head, met his gaze, and lifted one saucy brow. "At the saloon?"

"That's where a lot of folks are meeting up, from

66

the train. Townsfolk have people into their own homes to shelter them but folks're gathering at the saloon to talk about what happened. Feels better to share a misery, I guess." He shrugged. "Doc has been in and out, checking on as many as he can to be sure there aren't medical situations he needs to know about."

A slow nod. "That makes sense." She pulled her lip between her teeth for an instant before releasing it. "But I don't believe it's necessary to bother him. I'm hoping Georgina will recover. She's eaten well, walked around a bit, and we chatted. She's tired, though. I'm hoping rest will solve things for her."

He didn't have a lot of experience with women, but he knew enough to see this one had something heavy on her mind. "I see you're fretting over her. What exactly has you bothered?"

The sigh made him want to grab her and hold her close. So much sadness in one breath.

She met his gaze and shook her head. "Georgina doesn't remember a thing. Not about the train wreck, her cousin waiting for her in Laramie, her plan for the future...none of it." Her shoulders rose, then fell. "Nothing—not even her own name."

Chapter 13

Tate should have declined when Meg offered to heat bath water.

He should have considered propriety and her reputation before agreeing to climb into the big tin tub in his kitchen.

Another would have refused the offer to scrub his back when his work-battered shoulders, with their bruises and bumps, came into view.

That he did none of those things made him wonder what kind of man he'd grown to be, exactly. All his life he'd considered himself someone with good moral character, but now, as her warm hands glided over his skin, he couldn't be so sure.

His feelings for the woman, and for what she did with her soft, sudsy hands, exceeded the boundaries of their new relationship. His body reacted to her touch as if he'd been waiting all his life for her fingers to dance on his skin.

Meg knelt on a towel behind the tub, so he faced away from her. She'd heated enough water that he sat covered nearly to his chest. Bubbles danced below his nipples but the part of him that, even now, stiffened beneath her touch remained hidden from view.

"Did you get all of these bruises from rescuing us?" She ran a gentle finger across his right shoulder. "I don't believe I've ever seen this shade of purple before.

It looks painful."

He shook his head. "Some of them are from this past week. I've been moving inventory into the building and the barns out back. Sort of setting up shop, getting things ready to open for business."

The cloth she swept across the top of his back sent chills along his spine. How could something so ordinary feel this incredible? He had no idea, but if this were his last moment on earth, he'd go a happy man.

"I saw some crates. What kind of business are you starting?"

"Mining Supplies. There's some coal mining done out these ways and men need good tools to do the work. Safer if they're not cobbling cast-offs together to outfit themselves." He paused, remembering the stories he'd heard about mining accidents out west. If he had his way, none of that would happen in Wylder. "Men lose their lives, or worse, because they don't have reliable equipment."

Her hand reached around to dip the cloth in the tub. He watched her fingers plunge the square into the suds, then softly squeeze excess water out. Scant few inches separated those fingers from the part of him that throbbed beneath the surface.

Tate swallowed the groan that rose within him. Lord, but how much could a man take without losing his mind? Steam rose around them in the warm, darkened room. Every time Meg moved, a fresh wave of lavender swept up his nose, filling his head with thoughts that about drove him wild. Her fingertips were like a lover's kiss, soft and tender.

Her voice, so sweet and melodious, with an accent that made his heart smile, cut through the carnal thoughts filling his head. Hitching a breath, he turned to the right to meet her gaze over his shoulder.

And bumped noses with the woman.

Her eyes widened but she didn't back away.

They remained thusly for what felt like eternity but happened to be not more than three heartbeats.

His gaze dropped to her lips, inches from his own. This near, the scent of her enveloped him. A deep inhale brought the sweetness of her closer, but it did not satisfy him.

He wanted more.

Meg ran the tip of her tongue over her lower lip.

He watched, feeling heat grow with every second that passed. A grin lifted the corner of his mouth.

"What are you laughing at?" Her voice wobbled a bit, but her gaze didn't waver.

"I'm not laughing." He looked down at her mouth, then back to her eyes. "When you're considering something you put your teeth on your lower lip. It's charming."

An eyebrow rose. Another charming habit, he thought.

When she didn't reply, he lowered his voice and asked, "What were you thinking about?"

Meg sucked in a deep breath. She let it out in a long, slow exhale. Her voice a hint above a whisper, she said, "I wondered what it would be like to kiss you."

"I'm pondering the same thing."

Tate closed the distance between them and touched her lips with his own. She tasted as delectable as strawberries freshly plucked from the plant, still warm from the summer sun. They were his favorite food of all

70

time, always had been, but even the ripest fruit paled by comparison to the sweetest lips.

The kiss deepened. He nudged her mouth open with his tongue and when she offered entrance, he took it. With a hand dripping bathwater, he pulled her head closer and swept his tongue over hers. Their mouths danced the timeless steps that lovers shared, until they were both breathless.

When she leaned back he didn't hold her. His gut clenched, he wanted to keep her so much, but he released her. His gaze dropped to the luscious lips that still quivered before rising to her wide blue eyes.

"Everything you thought it would be?" He grinned, trying to catch his breath and hoping she wouldn't look too closely toward the bathwater. Most of the suds had flattened and he felt pretty sure the evidence of his desire poked near the water line.

Meg shook her head. A golden tendril danced on her shoulder. "No." Another small shake, as she pushed to her feet. "It was…much more."

Chapter 14

They shared a quiet meal. There were no more amorous moments. Both were polite and spoke about the current weather and Wylder. Neither mentioned the train derailment.

Meg cleared up afterward, content in the small yet well-equipped kitchen. She had located all the cookware and utensils earlier, while Tate moved freight and baggage from the accident scene. Now the cupboards were arranged in an orderly manner. She stored the dinner things where they belonged, gave the countertop one last wipe with a damp dishtowel, and looked around. Satisfied with her work, she hung the towel on a hook beside the sink and headed into the front room.

Cozy, overstuffed armchairs that had been in a side room now sat in the glow of the firelight. An ottoman, tufted and brightly patterned, sat between the two.

That he had made such an effort to offer her comfort touched her heart. The scene looked inviting and in that instant she realized that no one had ever gone to such trouble on her account.

A long moment to pause in the doorway. The scene mesmerized her with its simplicity and beauty. Its hominess tugged at her heartstrings. She wanted to stay in this moment for the rest of her life.

Tate sat in the chair with his back to her. Firelight

danced across the still-damp brown locks he'd cleaned so recently. Pinpricks of light showed the depths of the color, from dark brown to lighter, golden streaks.

No man's hair had caught her attention before but this one's did. And what covered his head wasn't the only thing that intrigued her. What lay beneath those brown strands, a man of honor and integrity who put his own life in jeopardy to save others. He seemed like a dream, something tossed from the deepest part of her heart and mind and turned into flesh and blood.

He had been kind to her and Georgina despite not knowing them. He had been nicer to her than the man who sired her had ever been.

How to repay someone for showing compassion like none she'd seen before?

She clasped her hands at her waist and walked into the room. He made to stand but she waved him down. "No, please, don't get up. You worked hard all day; you must be tired." She swept her hand toward the empty chair. "Mind if I sit?"

He half-rose and nodded. "Please, do."

She did, so he lowered himself back into his seat. A tiny grimace twisted his mouth for an instant before he assumed a peaceful demeanor again. His body hurt, then.

When he had been in the kitchen bathing, she could have stolen a look at the leg that pained him so. It crossed her mind, but she didn't do it. A man should have some privacy afforded him in his own home. But she wondered what had happened to him, what injured him so that his handsome face twisted when the pain hit him.

She searched her mind for a topic of conversation

that might be engaging or fascinate her host. Her lack of social graces she attributed to the Reverend. If they were in a church she'd know exactly what to say and do, but here, out in the world, she felt lost.

Tate saved her. Again.

"I see you tidied up the place today. It looks nice, but you didn't have to do that."

She had put the kitchen to rights and the area out here by the fireplace had been swept and dusted. Crates from the center of the room she'd pushed to the sides, and a large, braided rug from the back hallway now sat in the middle of the open floorspace.

"It gave me something to do. I would have unpacked your crates, but I didn't know where to put things." She had peeked at the contents of some to see whether she'd be able to move them. They were filled with miner's hats, axes, and lanterns—and where did one stow items like that? "If you tell me where you want everything, I'll take care of it tomorrow."

He stared across the space at her. She knew enough about men, thanks to the Reverend, to see he mulled something over. And she also knew better than to interrupt a man consumed by the act of thinking.

Her mother had told her that most men couldn't do more than one thing at a time, so she gave Tate quiet to use his mind.

But Mother had also advised that men thought with what lay below their waists and there was no food in sight. Maybe it proved more difficult to think without a meal, so she settled back and decided to give the man in the other chair some extra time. For thinking, of course.

To her surprise, he answered quickly.

"You don't need to take care of anything, although

I appreciate that you want to help." He gestured with one hand to the large, almost empty room. "As you can tell, I'm in the process of moving in and setting up. But you're here to rest, stay safe, get stronger after your ordeal. You shouldn't trouble yourself with unpacking or sweeping."

"I don't mind." And the truth of it? She really didn't.

Firelight danced on the floor at their feet and made the shadows in the corners of the room come alive. Snow fell outdoors, heat bloomed between them…and Meg realized she'd never been more content.

Did other people feel this all the time? At ease and safe?

She thought they might. Then she gave herself a mental shake. This moment would pass, and she'd be back on the streets again. She'd best not get used to feeling this good.

"Tell me about yourself, Meg."

Uh oh.

What could she say?

As if he read her mind, Tate added, "And the truth, please. It seems a night for sharing secrets, doesn't it? I've got a few I need to get off my chest. Maybe you've got one or two to tell, too."

She couldn't argue, it did feel like they were cocooned from the world, safe and secure in this bubble of contentment. It might be the only chance she would ever have to tell her truth, the one she'd never spoken aloud.

What did she have to lose?

She took a deep breath. Better to begin with the most important fact, that she would never return east to the life she fled.

"I left the Reverend back in Boston. He has no idea where I've gone, and I have no intention of ever seeing him again." She paused, and locked her gaze with Tate's. "Ever."

"Your husband?" His voice held no judgment.

"No. The Reverend is the man my mother married, the one who planted the seed that became me."

"Your father, then?"

She shook her head and turned to face the fire. "I have never called him that and I won't, not ever. The man didn't know how to love anyone—he gave up the right to be called that the first time he hit my mother. And that, I've been told, began when he found out she carried his child."

A log popped and a tiny shower of sparks flew about in the hearth.

"I'm sorry." He reached a hand out into the space between them. When she took it, he gave her a small squeeze. "I'm truly sorry. It sounds as if you had a hard life. Do you think it's better now that you're not in Boston anymore, not with that man who did not deserve a beautiful daughter?"

She inhaled sharply and held the breath. Did she think this a better life? One spent homeless and on the run?

And her plan for the future—it included something the Reverend would have a seizure over if he ever found out. Her only option, a woman alone and without means, as far as she could tell. She'd never tried anything like it before but how hard could it be, really?

Pushing the thought of what lay ahead from her mind, she nodded. "Yes, my life is much better now."

"I'm glad to hear it." He squeezed a second time. "Do you want to tell the whole story? I'm a good listener and we've got nowhere to go and nothing else to do. It's been my experience that once a story is told, the teller can walk away from it without looking back. Leave it to the world, as it were." He turned to her, his face serious in the firelight. "I'm willing to be your world if you're ready to tell your story."

She took a second deep breath.

Now or never, she thought. She plunged in, before she could talk herself out of letting the story out of the confinement she'd kept it in.

"The Reverend had us both under his thumb. Neither my mother nor I were allowed to do ordinary things, the way other families did. No, he said we were sinners and needed his help to redeem ourselves." She swallowed hard, determined to tell it once, walk away from it, and never look back, the way Tate suggested. "He had all sorts of methods for disciplining us when we didn't do something that pleased him. And honestly, the fact that we exist displeased him, so life had a hardness to it."

They sat in silence for a few moments.

Their hands were still joined, and she hoped he wouldn't release hers. The feel of his palm against hers provided strength and she appreciated the support.

"Your mother? Is she still in Boston?"

Pain smashed into her, a wave so hard that had they not been sitting she would have fallen to her knees.

"The fire eight years ago, the one that burned acres in the city...she had gone out to get a certain kind of fabric he preferred his handkerchiefs be made of. She got caught in the inferno and never came home that day." A shiver ran through her. Her heart still bled, raw from the loss. "He killed her, with his ridiculous demands. Had she not been there she'd be here, with me, now."

That plan, the one they'd worked on for so long, also got burned in the Boston fire.

Tate's question came gently. "She would have left him, too?"

"Of course. We were only waiting for the right moment to run." She gave him a small smile. "I found one—so I ran."

Chapter 15

The building's upstairs living space had been designed to accommodate a family.

The large front bedroom, two additional sleeping chambers, a parlor and a second smaller kitchen made the space functional, but it retained an air of coziness about it. Fireplaces to warm each area. A third-floor attic offered room for expansion.

That the previous owner built the space for the family he hoped to one day fill it with showed in every extra little touch. The bedrooms all had built-in closets rather than the standard wall hooks in most rooms Tate had seen. Nooks for reading and alcoves for children's adventures dotted the interior.

It sat hard on Tate's heart that the man's dreams had been shattered when his bride succumbed to childbearing difficulties. That the babe had been lost, as well, only added to the sorrow. He couldn't imagine how any man survived a calamity of that magnitude. He prayed he never found out.

The man's loss had benefitted Tate when he sold it all at a fraction of the proper going rate and headed out west. One man's broken dream became another's good fortune.

He didn't mind sleeping in one of the smaller bedrooms while his guests occupied the marital bedchamber. He'd only been using it because it came fully furnished and offered a view of the street.

Lying in bed on his back, the circle of light thrown by the kerosene lamp cutting the darkness, he took a deep breath and tried to make sense of the past few days. So much had happened, his mind felt as scrambled as one of the eggs Meg dropped into the breakfast skillet.

The woman's story hit his heart—almost as hard as he wanted to hit the Reverend. He'd never understood how a man could live with himself when he mistreated a woman. It made no sense. Everyone knew they were angels on earth, to be cherished and protected.

In the dim room, his hand curled into a fist. Clenching the muscles caused pain, so he unfurled his fingers but in his mind, he kept a fist ready for the scoundrel who hurt the delicate creature he'd rescued from the wreck.

Yes, he'd love the chance to throw a punch at the man who fathered the woman sleeping across the hall from him.

He ran one hand through his hair and pushed his book aside with the other. Too much in his head to read tonight. When he leaned over to blow out the lamp, a knock came at the door.

He wondered if he'd imagined the sound. Then, two more light taps.

"Yes?" He sat up in bed and reached for the shirt hanging on the bedpost.

The door opened and a flickering candle, held aloft, entered the room. Meg raised it so high her face looked ringed in light. She wore a white nightdress with a matching shawl draped across her shoulders.

"May I come in?" She spoke softly but her voice sounded loud in the quiet room. "Am I disturbing you?"

"Of course." He shrugged into his shirt and thought about rising from the bed but she'd caught him in his long johns. His trousers lay across a chair on the far side of the room. "And no, you're not a disturbance. Is everything okay? Georgina—does she need a doctor because I can go for him if she's taken a bad turn."

She closed the door behind her and crossed the room. Her bare feet were silent on the floorboards. When she stood beside the bed, the head shake she gave sent golden locks tumbling across her slender shoulders.

"She's fine. Sound asleep and hopefully by tomorrow she'll remember who she is." She placed the candleholder on the edge of the fireplace mantel and wrapped her arms beneath the shawl. "I hope you don't mind my coming here. If you want me to leave, I will."

He tried to be an upstanding man where women were concerned but he was, after all, only human. He hadn't been this close to a scantily dressed female in longer than he could remember.

And the scent of lavender danced around her like a summer meadow, so sweet and pure it made him want to bury his face in her neck and inhale the aroma of the woman.

"I don't want you to leave." He glanced around the room, mindful of his pant-less condition. There were few comforts here. He imagined this room had been destined for future use, a nursery perhaps, and never fully furnished. "I'm sorry there isn't a comfortable chair for you to sit on."

They stared at each other for a long moment. She

took a deep breath, held it in her lungs, and let it out very slowly before nodding to the bed.

"I can sit beside you, if you don't mind."

His mouth went dry. Maybe he should pinch himself, to see if he dreamed, because this seemed too perfect to be real. But if he did that, and this didn't turn out to be part of his imagination, he'd appear dim-witted, the last thing he wanted to do.

Instead, he held his hand to the side closest to where she stood. "I don't mind at all."

The woman had other ideas. He'd thought she'd perch on the edge. That idea vanished as he watched her move across the space.

She left the circle of light, walked around the bottom of the bed, and pulled the blankets on the other side back. He felt, more than saw, her slip onto the mattress and settle back against the pillow on her side.

Her side. How fast that happened!

His mind raced. And his body heated. The scent of her filled the room now, so pure and clean that he could barely resist taking her in his arms and crushing her to his chest.

As he wondered what to say, she slipped across the sheet and nestled against his side. He gazed down into her face and fell into the depths of her gentle blue eyes.

She took another deep inhale, followed by a long, slow exhale. "Tate, will you have me?"

He opened his eyes as wide as they would go. No woman had ever invited such a thing—and he hadn't expected it now.

Did she know what she asked of him? Of course, she did—she must, mustn't she? His mind ran circles but before he could formulate a reply she moved still closer.

And kissed him. Her lips parted and her tongue swirled over his, urging them to grant entrance. When he did, she deepened the kiss, coaxing his face closer with a soft hand pressed to the back of his neck.

He groaned. His self-restraint at its breaking point, he reached for her and wrapped his arms around her warm body. He lifted her onto his lap and twined his fingers in the soft cascade trailing down her back.

Her fingers dropped low on his chest, trailing a line down the front of his shirt and unbuttoning it as they went. When she'd opened every button, she slid her hands beneath the worn fabric and ran them over his skin. Her touch, whisper-soft and so tender, made goosebumps rise on his arms.

Not the only part of him that rose.

It quickly became impossible to conceal his desire. It throbbed thick and hard between them. A fleeting thought that she might be put off by his arousal flew from his mind when she rocked against him, and he felt the heat at the apex of her thighs.

"Meg—" Her name came as a prayer, furtive and heartfelt. He felt things he'd never felt before, emotions he'd not thought possible. With her in his arms he felt complete—and he didn't want to let her go. Not now—not ever.

She swept a slow line of kisses down his neck, lingering on his throat beneath his jaw. Her mouth drove him to the edge of madness—in a good way, the way a man dreamed of being sent.

He nudged her face to his own and placed a hand on her cheek. Her eyes—his need to see them beat an insistent hammer inside his head. When their gazes met, she offered a tiny smile.

Amazing that during the heat of passion, she could bring those beautiful lips into the perfect bow shape. They were swollen from their kissing, but that made them even more beautiful. He shook his head. "You are a surprise, aren't you? A wonderful, warm, welcome one." He touched his lips to hers, a quick nibble before he tilted his head back. "You know what you're doing to me, don't you?"

Never taking her gaze from his, she reached between them, pushed his garment aside, and took him in her hand. As if to show that she did, indeed, recognize the effect she had on him, she gave him a gentle squeeze. Then she began to move her hand up and down his length.

When she lifted the edge of her nightdress he needed no further confirmation that she consented to what they were doing and more importantly, to what they were about to do. He ran a hand along the firm flesh of her outer thigh, then traced a path on the sensitive inner side. She shivered against him as he touched the delicate folds that were beneath his fingertip, slick with need.

A moan escaped her, low and long, and sounding pulled from the depths of her soul.

Meg rose above him and placed her body over his, angling him to fit into her.

She met his gaze and placed her mouth over his, kissing him with so much passion that all thought left his mind—almost. It hit him that when she lowered herself onto him, the smooth slide he'd anticipated did not happen. Resistance met his throbbing flesh but his instinct, to pull back, was hampered by their positions.

She sat astride and when he would have put space between them, she pressed hard against him until finally he entered her.

"Ah!" Her gasp on his lips as she stilled made his heart stutter.

Tate put a hand behind her neck and urged her to meet his gaze. When she did, he saw the truth.

"Why didn't you tell me?" He would have done this so much differently had he known. "I didn't know, Meg. I would have made sure you were ready, made it easier for you, if I knew."

She shook her head. "You've made it perfect. More than I imagined it would be, so please, let's not speak of it." She gave a little wiggle on him and that she didn't wince when she did gave him hope that she didn't feel pain. "There's more to this, isn't there? Can you show me the rest?"

He kissed her then, tenderly and without any thought to finishing the act.

They had the entire night ahead of them and he intended to make every minute count. He needed to show her how beautiful lovemaking could be.

Before the sun rose, he'd shown her twice.

Chapter 16

"Georgina, would you like some more eggs?" Meg brought the skillet to the table and prepared to spoon some onto the other's plate, but she got waved away.

"No, thank you. I am more than satisfied by what I've eaten." The woman swept a look toward Tate, then met her gaze. "You've both been so kind. And you've taken such good care of me. I don't know how I will ever repay you."

Tate nodded when she offered him the last of the eggs. He moved back to let her close and she felt him watching her as she refilled his plate. Heat rose in her cheeks, fueled by the nearness of the man and the knowledge that he'd seen her in the throes of passion.

She wondered what he thought of her this morning. Truth be told, she imagined he took her for a loose woman. A common whore, perhaps. And that fit, because she planned to go into the profession once she found her way to a safe place.

"Thank you." His tone held no sign of disgust so maybe he didn't think too poorly of her, after all.

"You're welcome." She took the skillet back to the stove, grabbed the coffee pot and a slice of wood to serve as a trivet, and returned to the table. When she sat, she placed the pot in the center within reach of all three of them. She picked up her fork. Her plate didn't hold much anymore but she had a powerful appetite this morning and planned to eat every morsel.

Who knew sexual relations could stir up such hunger?

"You don't need to repay me. Why, I bet every home in Wylder has taken in folks from the train. It's what people do in a bad situation, we help each other." He looked from one woman to the other. "It's my pleasure having you both here and you're welcome to stay as long as you like."

She kept her gaze on the food but nodded. "That's kind of you."

Georgina sighed, the sound so loud it could not be ignored.

"What's wrong?" She checked the other woman's color. She looked fine, not at all pale the way she had been right after she'd hit her head. Her cheeks bloomed and her eyes were clear and until now she'd seemed content to be with them. "Do you feel unwell?"

With a second dramatic sigh, the woman put one arm up and placed her wrist against her forehead. "I do not know who I am. How can I feel well under these circumstances?"

Meg and Tate exchanged glances.

Words failed her. She had tried to nudge her friend's memory, recounting their train journey, the books they'd chatted about and even the meals they'd shared—all to no reward. Nothing brought a glimmer of recollection or any assurance she believed the tales.

He cleared his throat. "Maybe seeing some of the other passengers will bring back a memory. I know a lot of folks are spending their days at the Five Star, talking about what went on and waiting for news from the rail line."

"News about what?" Her appetite disappeared. What if the Reverend tracked her down? The fear he'd find her never strayed far from her mind. "What would they have to say to anyone? It's still snowing hard so they can't possibly be coming to repair the line, can they?"

"No, nothing like that. I don't think anyone really expects to hear anything. I guess they're gathering to feel some kind of security, I suppose."

That made sense. She looked over her shoulder toward the window. Snow still fell heavily.

"How far is it to town?"

"Not very. We're this side of the tracks, next to Miss Addie's place. A short ride and we'll be right on Wylder Street, in the center of everything." He put his fork down and stood. "If you ladies would like, I'm happy to escort you to town. I have some business at the mercantile, so whenever you're ready, we can get a move on."

She met Georgina's gaze. "Think you're up for a ride?"

The other woman shrugged. "Why not? It might be fun to see where we ended up." A small smile made her expression less gloomy. "Besides, we've already been pummeled by the snowstorm. What more can it do to us?"

Chapter 17

Tate stopped at the livery to have a word about replacing the work animal he'd lost. There were none available but the man who owned the place promised to keep his ears open for talk of a good horse for sale.

He climbed back into the wagon and set the one that remained in motion.

Beside him, the woman he'd held in his arms until a few hours ago sat as serenely as if they hadn't enjoyed each other all night long. A mystery to him how she acted as if nothing happened. He forced his mind to stay on guiding the horse when it tried to stray into carnal territory.

He heard echoes of her moans in his head. They affected him, despite the cold temperature of the snowy morning.

How a memory could give him an erection in the middle of a snowstorm went against every ounce of logic he possessed but the truth could not be denied. At least he didn't have to climb down for a few minutes yet. Time enough to gather his wits and get himself under control—or so he hoped.

Snow blew into their faces, making conversation impossible.

The women wanted to see the collected baggage. Both hoped to find some of their own belongings, and he agreed that sounded like a fine idea, so they stopped at the church first.

He helped them alight, and they went inside.

Just his bad luck, Violet met them at the door. The one woman he hoped to avoid, standing right before him looking every inch the disapproving schoolteacher when she caught sight of him. Her hands clasped at her waist, her mouth set in a thin line, and her brows furrowed. The intriguing violet eyes looking ready to throw daggers if he stepped a toe out of line.

"I thought you'd be at the schoolhouse." He spoke without thinking and as soon as the statement left his mouth he wished he could pull it back.

"My sister Lily is with the children. There are only a few, mostly from the train since the weather is so bad." She looked to the two women beside him and nodded. "Are you ladies from the train, too?"

"We are. I'm Meg and this is my friend, Georgina. Tate rescued us. I'm sure we would have perished without him."

Georgina added, "Oh, yes. From what I'm told, he carried my unconscious body from a flaming train car. I owe my life to this man." She placed a hand on his arm and smiled.

Violet had been raised in South Carolina and she and her sisters had a strict southern upbringing. Being from the state himself and having been a patient under her mother's care during the war, he knew the look she gave his two guests concealed a lot. He saw it in her eyes, that she would have made a remark of some sort if they were alone but kept her tongue instead.

She obviously hadn't forgiven him for being intoxicated. More likely, she still had a bee in her bonnet about his stealing that kiss. And he couldn't blame her. He had been wrong.

But he did not regret his actions. Kissing Violet showed him that he didn't love her, not in the way he'd believed. It left him free to have feelings for another.

Like Meg. He'd only known her a short time, but it felt as if she'd been in his life forever. Maybe near-death experiences did that for folks, brought them close in a heartbeat. He couldn't tell, but if that's what went on between them he had a grateful heart.

"Well, that's not a surprise. Tate is quite the gentleman." Violet smiled and waved a hand to the room behind her. "Are you ladies looking for your belongings?"

"We are." Meg glanced at the chaotic scene. Bags of every size and description, some intact while others looked worse for having been in the wreck, piled high. "Oh, dear. I hope ours are here."

"Why, Tate Taylor! Violet told me you left Wylder."

He turned and came face to face with another of the Bloom sisters. Pansy looked as he remembered, cheerful and full of life.

He dipped his chin and shook his head. "Why, you're the spittin' image of your mother, aren't you? It's good to see you but when did you arrive in town? You weren't here when I left."

The woman reached out and put a hand on his jacket above his heart. "Well, it looks like you and I have some catchin' up to do. When I arrived, when you returned…sounds like we'll have a fine chat, doesn't it?" She turned to the other women. "Looking to claim your things, ladies? I can help you search if you'd like."

Pansy put out a hand and led the two toward the

stacks. He thought he should help but when Violet didn't move, he didn't, either.

They stood in silence for a moment. There were others in the room, looking through the satchels, boxes, and valises that appeared to be mostly personal belongings. He wondered where the freight had gone. One of his crates hadn't arrived home with him and he needed to track it down.

But now did not seem like the ideal time to inquire about missing explosives.

He twirled his hat in his hands, working the brim as he searched for an opening.

No way around it. Time to swallow his pride.

He turned to Violet and cleared his throat. She met his gaze, and it didn't seem as stern now. Maybe helping damsels in distress took him up a notch in her estimation. He certainly hoped so.

"I'm sorry for the way I behaved. My bad manners and, um, well…" How to apologize for stealing a kiss that gave him the freedom to realize he didn't love her? He wasn't sorry for finding out that information, only regretted taking what she hadn't freely offered.

Whiskey was not his friend.

"Liberty-taking?"

He sighed, grateful she helped him along. "Yes, ma'am, my liberty-taking was completely out of line. I apologize for my terrible behavior and I hope you'll find it in your heart to forgive me."

The schoolteacher tapped her toe against the floorboards. She seemed poised to ask him something but shook her head. "I forgive you. I've done some thinking about what happened and I've talked it over with Thomas—"

"Excuse me? You mean you told him I—" He looked around at the crowd inside the church and dropped his voice to a whisper. "You told Thomas I kissed you?"

Her brow furrowed again. "No, of course not. I told him you were drunk, in the morning, no less. And he pointed out that the scene at the train derailment could send any man to the bottle. He reminded me that he'd taken a nip that first night, too."

Well, he never expected Harvey to help him out, but he appreciated that he had.

He couldn't help but ask the question that meant so much to him. "Are you happy with him, then? It's been two years and you're still keepin' company. That must mean you get along, doesn't it?"

Her stormy countenance gentled instantly. The grip her fingers held on each other eased. Her brow released its furrows, turning her forehead smooth again. And her lips, so expressive and, he now knew, soft, moved from their displeased straight line.

The smile on her face told him all he needed to know. "I'm very happy with him. He's everything I've ever wanted and so much more." She hesitated, then put a hand on his forearm. "I hope that you find the same kind of love someday, too. I really do."

He swept his gaze over the room, past the other people rummaging for belongings, by the stacks of mismatched luggage, until he found the only object in the place that sent his heart beating double time.

Meg happened to look up and their gazes met. She waved, he nodded, and then he turned to Violet. "I do, too."

Chapter 18

Meg tucked her reticule close to the front of her coat. Locating it in the stacks of belongings inside the church had been a blessing. One of the few possessions she had that belonged to her mother, it would always be a treasure.

When Pansy Bloom held it up she felt her heart jump for joy. She'd described it to the other woman but hadn't expected that anyone would find it in the jumble. It had been hard to restrain herself. She'd wanted to hug her for recovering it.

Her meager funds were thankfully intact inside the bag. They were the only thing that separated her from living in an alley somewhere, so having them returned gave her a small sense of security. They wouldn't go far but she planned on finding employment right along, although now that she and Tate shared a night she wondered how she would move on from the experience. Her heart hurt when she considered leaving him.

No time for thinking about any of that so she pushed it from her mind and focused on the positive. Like the funds inside her mother's reticule and the luggage that held her worldly goods. Both were back with her, as were Georgina's things. What more could one hope for?

Wylder's residents proved trustworthy, more so than those she left behind in Boston. There one looked over a shoulder constantly, wary of being set upon by ruffians. Since she'd heard stories of nefarious frontiersmen and wild ranch hands, she expected to spend every moment in the west fighting for survival. That her life had been saved and her meager belongings salvaged felt nothing short of a miracle.

And that she'd met the man seated beside her in the wagon only added to the amazement coursing through her veins. She chanced a glance at him. Her emotions jumped at the sight of his chiseled features. He focused on getting the horse and wagon through the snowstorm, so his gaze sat squarely on the white mess before them, but she remembered the vivid blue eyes that had looked on her through the night, and felt butterflies low in her belly.

The man touched her in ways she never expected—and she didn't mean on only a physical aspect. No, he touched her soul.

She would need to get over letting anyone into that space if she was going to go through with her employment plan. It wouldn't do to allow every man she serviced to place a fingertip on her heart. She needed to figure out how to keep that from happening.

"The mercantile is just ahead." The wind nearly swallowed his voice, but he leaned close and spoke loudly. "I'm gonna pull up right in front and let you ladies out. Then I'll park the wagon and meet you inside."

She squeezed his arm to let him know she heard, then put her mouth beside Georgina's ear and repeated his words.

It eased her mind to see her companion out of bed and on her feet. Hopefully, her memory would return soon.

When the wagon stopped she signaled that they could climb to the snowy ground unassisted. The other woman scrambled down first and then she followed. When her feet touched, snow swirled up near her knees but once she reached the wooden walkway things changed. It had been shoveled.

They made a rush for the front door and fell inside, shaking snow from their shoulders, swishing it from their skirt hems, and stamping their feet to free their boots of the white stuff.

Meg looked up. The mercantile building spread both wide and deep, one of the biggest shops she'd seen. In Boston there were many small shops, one after the next it seemed, in most neighborhoods. Specialty stores were popular. This one, with its vast floor space and rows upon rows of goods, looked to offer anything and everything anyone might need.

She didn't know where to investigate first.

Georgina linked her arm and tugged her forward. "We should get some foodstuffs. Tate is feeding us, after all. We shouldn't empty his pantry."

The paltry amount of money she possessed wouldn't go far. Her friend seemed to sense her hesitation because she leaned close and lowered her voice. "I have funds to pay for this—and don't deny me the pleasure. You two saved my life and cared for me when I couldn't. The least I can do is buy supplies." A table stacked high with wicker baskets stood to the side of the doorway. She grabbed two and handed one over. "Here. Help me—and don't be shy about putting whatever you want in the basket. There's a big wad of cash in my reticule so apparently I'm not lacking for resources. And it's Christmas week. Let's shop!"

The mercantile teemed with friendly faces. She had no idea who lived in town and who were train survivors, but all seemed glad to browse the aisles. Many women smiled and said hello, while men dipped their chins. Whether the spirit of Christmas or joy over being alive touched everyone, she didn't know. But this Wylder welcome brought tightness to Meg's chest and raised a lump in her throat.

"What do you think Tate fancies? Oranges or apples?" Her companion held up one of each and gave her a questioning look. She sniffed both, then handed them over so Meg obligingly brought each to her nose. A whiff of summer, if ever there were one. "They're both enticing so let's get some of each. I'll grab apples and you can select oranges."

The open baskets holding fruit made it a snap to choose. They moved on and picked up pantry basics, including a tin of Arbuckle's coffee and some sugar. Georgina seemed unconcerned about the cost of goods and piled her basket full.

She nodded toward Meg, whose basket held little more than the fruit. "Please, I mean it when I say put anything you'd like in that basket. You know our host better than I do. Get whatever you think would make that man smile—other than you, that is."

Her eyebrows went up so fast she didn't have time to stop them. The Reverend believed expressive facial features were the devil's work. She'd learned early to control hers in order to avoid the strap he wielded. Her defenses were down since she'd freed herself of his hateful opinions, and now she didn't try to hide her surprise.

"Whatever are you talking about?" Color rose in her cheeks and she pulled her brows back into place. "I don't know what you mean by that."

"Oh, don't you?"

The teasing tone brought a smile. She'd been so afraid her friend would die. This lively exchange touched her heart. It reminded her of the carefree hours they'd spent on the train before the crash.

"I most certainly do not." She grinned, then added, "Well, maybe I do. He is nice, isn't he?"

"Well, considering we wouldn't be standing here if not for him, I'd say he's nice." Georgina swept her fingers through a bushel of walnuts. "Think he'd like these? Wait, don't answer. We'll get some and if he doesn't we can hide them in a loaf of sweet bread."

The way the other woman deftly chose nuts, squeezing each one before adding it to a small paper sack, showed her comfort around baking supplies. And it hit Meg that she'd chosen fruit without hesitation, too.

"Georgina, I think you must be a good cook. Or at least, a baker."

She watched as the idea settled with her friend. Finally, she nodded. "You might be right. I feel more comfortable here surrounded by food than I have since I woke up. And when we were in the kitchen this morning making breakfast I felt at home."

Before she could reply she heard footsteps on the floor behind her. She looked up as Tate stopped by her side. He held out his hands and took her basket, then Georgina's. He held them as if they were filled with feathers instead of supplies.

"We're picking up some necessities." The other

woman gestured to the shelves around them. "Is there anything special you'd like for dinner?"

He shook his head. "No, ma'am. I'm not too fussy. Whatever lands on the table is fine by me."

"Easy to please?" Meg couldn't resist the tiny observation. She smiled. "Is that true?"

He tilted his head and met her gaze and it felt as if the entire shop around them faded away, as if they were the only two people in the place and nothing else mattered. "Hard to please about certain things, but food ain't one of them. Selective, though, when it comes to…um, well, let's say I'm choosy when it matters."

Words eluded her so she glanced down at her toes for a moment. When she looked up, he peered into the basket she'd filled, and a big smile crossed his face. "I don't know how you figured that I have a fondness for oranges."

"Oh, do you?"

"Mmm hmm. I have a taste for the sweeter bits of life."

Before she could reply a woman strode up to them. Older, with graying hair and a work-worn expression, she brightened when she smiled up at Tate.

"Why, it's good to see you back in Wylder! I bet Violet's glad to see you. I know she missed you when you left so suddenly."

Tate looked as if he'd rather be anywhere but in the mercantile, so Meg took a step toward the counter where a tall man with a kind face and striking eyes stood waiting to cash them out.

"Miss Gertie, you're looking well. Thank you for the warm welcome, ma'am. I'm happy to be back but if you'll excuse us, I've got more errands to run before we head home."

She and Georgina moved closer to the counter, with Tate following, but the woman hadn't finished with him.

She called, in a voice that could be heard across the entire shop, "Well, as long as I see you on Christmas Eve at the town party. Violet and the children will have a celebration to close the year on a high note. Bring your two lady friends, too. The more, the merrier!"

Chapter 19

Now that they'd claimed their belongings they had little more to do but wait for the snowstorm to end.

Since Tate seemed pleased to have them stay with him, they could see no reason to leave. Gratitude swept through Meg when Georgina agreed it seemed the most logical course of action. Their days settled into a quiet pattern, almost as if they were family. She welcomed the new experience. With the Reverend, nothing felt this peaceful.

It became clear they had interrupted the man in setting up his shop, so as the snow piled high outside, they helped him get the situation sorted out. Rows of shelves went down the center of the space. Hooks from the wooden ceiling beams were screwed into place. The floorboards got scrubbed and inner panes of glass on the wide storefront windows washed until they shone.

She had never been this happy.

Her days were spent working on the shop and her nights...well, those hours of passion opened her mind, body, and soul like she'd never dreamed possible.

Now she understood why whorehouses stayed in business. Humans needed companionship like what she and Tate shared. Although she couldn't imagine how she would do the things they did with other men when the time came, but she pushed that from her mind and concentrated on what she had now. These days would pass quickly and never come again. She didn't want to waste them worrying about the future.

She glanced over at Georgina. The woman grew stronger by the day, more like the woman on the train than the nearly lifeless one they'd managed to bring to this safe spot. Sometimes she acted as if she remembered things, poised to say something that might show a connection with her past, but she never did.

Now she stacked gloves on a shelf, separating them by size and color. Brown and black, a case of each, had come in on a freight car with their train. Georgina worked steadily, not engaging in chatter but doing every task assigned without comment. Meg wondered what she thought about so quietly but did not want to intrude by asking.

Besides, she had her own thoughts to consider. She looked over at the man who occupied most of them.

He wrapped ropes into tidy bundles and hung them from hooks on the far wall. She watched his biceps ripple as he used his forearm to wind the heavy coils. A shiver went up her spine as she conjured a mental image of those arms, uncovered and holding the naked man above her as they turned hour upon nighttime hour into glorious splendor.

As if he felt her watching him, the object of her consideration turned his head and met her gaze. He gave her a small grin and winked, which sent the butterflies that now constantly danced in her belly into a frenzy.

"How's it going over there? Are you sure you can get those lanterns up without any help?" As ever, the man's voice slid over her ears and into her head like a golden silk ribbon, so smooth and beautiful that she sighed when he spoke.

"I'm fine, thanks."

He'd brought a stepladder over and placed it below the beams where he'd hung hooks. She had spent the last hour unpacking two large crates of lanterns. They arrived with their globes wrapped separately so she'd put them together and now planned to hang them.

She grabbed three lanterns in one hand and put one foot on the bottom rung.

Climbing a ladder had not been a skill the Reverend thought she ought to learn so this new experience unsettled her. She put her weight on the foot, but the ladder leaned so she slid her toes further onto the step and tried again. It worked, no tilt, so she put her other foot onto the step and began to climb.

A thought shot through her. If she could do this, she could do anything, right?

"You okay over there?" The other woman looked up from her gloves. "I can help. I'm not afraid of heights."

She nearly scowled at her friend but since she knew she meant well she restrained herself. "I'm not frightened, either." Standing near the top step made the ladder wobble a smidgen but she swallowed her apprehension and reached out an arm. The first lantern slipped right onto its hook, so she placed the second one beside it. The third hung out of reach but she angled the wire hanger on the lantern and leaned to the right. It caught the ceiling hook, so she released her hold.

Too late, she realized the ladder tilted far from center. For one long breathless moment she hung in mid-air, with two of the wooden feet off the floor while she waited to fall. Then, the thing tipped so far that her toes slipped from the rung.

Tate's strong arms caught her before she hit the floor. The ladder crashed beside them, but he cradled her against his chest and carried her clear.

"Oh! How did you do that?" She gazed up into his eyes. "It happened so fast!"

He could have put her feet on the ground, but he held her and walked across the room until they were beside the belly stove.

"You're shaking." He gave her a soft squeeze before he lowered her feet to the floor. "Have you ever climbed anything before?"

She didn't consider lying to him and shook her head.

"Why didn't you say so? You could've broken your neck falling off that ladder." His words were strong, but his gaze turned tender. "You scared the heck out of me."

"I'm sorry. I wanted you to be impressed by all the things I can do." She lifted her shoulders, then let them fall. "It's silly, I know, but the Reverend never considered me good enough for anything important and I wanted to prove myself."

As she said the words she heard how ridiculous they sounded. But she also felt the child within her, the little girl who spent her whole life trying to prove herself worthy of love.

Tate ran a gentle finger over her temple and pushed a dangling lock of hair off her face. She must have lost a hair pin when she fell. His caress made her think she might leave a pin or two from every updo, so he'd touch her this way.

"I'm not much good with fancy words but I hoped you knew by now that you don't need to prove anything to me." He paused and swept a lazy fingertip over her cheek. It sent shivers up her spine. "I am thoroughly impressed with you, dear Meg. Please don't go climbing on my account. I don't want to see you get hurt—not now, not ever."

He looked ready to kiss her when a sharp knock came from the front of the building. She stepped away, closer to the stove, while he went to the door and looked out.

Two men stood on the wide front walkway. They sheltered from the worst of the snow by the overhang, but both appeared to have been in the weather for a bit. She saw a pair of horses with bedrolls on their saddles tied at the hitching post.

Tate unlocked the door and pulled it in a few inches. "We're not open for business, fellas. And I don't think there's much mining bein' done in this weather, anyhow."

"Taylor, we've tracked you from California clear across the frontier into this snowstorm and we aim to have a conversation with you." He unbuttoned his jacket to reveal the guns holstered on his hips. "We can do it nice and easy—I see you got womenfolk in there and I don't mean to disrespect them—or we can do it hard. Your choice."

The male voice that replied sounded weary. It also held a callousness to it that reminded her of the Reverend.

Tate took a deep breath. "Give me ten minutes to get my horse saddled up. We'll have this conversation in my lawyer's office if it's all the same to you.

Addison Merriweather, he's right in town, five minutes from here."

The man nodded. "We've come this far. Another few minutes either way ain't gonna make one lick of difference."

Chapter 20

Relief fortified Tate when he saw the glow of light coming from inside Addison Merriweather's office. Finding him at his desk when the wind howled, and the snow blew sideways instead of at home snugged up beside a roaring fire turned out to be blind luck.

He'd had a lot of good turns lately, most importantly finding Meg. He hoped he hadn't depleted his store of good fortune.

He knew they were bound to catch up eventually but still, it unnerved him to see the five-point silver stars pinned to the men's vests. U.S. Marshals come all this way, as if he were an outlaw.

Which, by some accounts, he might very well be.

Addison looked up from his desk when Tate stepped inside and stamped his feet on the floorboards already puddled with melted snow. The marshals brought up the rear, with the last man in struggling to close the door against the powerful frigid wind.

The attorney looked more like a ranch hand than a man who spent his days surrounded by books and his nose buried in legal documents. Wide shoulders and biceps the size of hams showed how he spent his free time. Talk about town, that he owned a substantial parcel of land with a stream that yielded gold flakes, and a cavern where he mined for iron deposits, explained his physical appearance.

They were the reasons Tate had chosen his representation. Mining got in a man's blood in a way few could understand. And miners looked out for each other.

"Well, didn't expect to see you so soon." When the man stood the room felt smaller. He held out his hand and after they shook, he tucked his thumbs under the top of the gun belt he wore low over his hips and rocked back on his heels. "Some friends of yours, Tate?"

The one closest to the desk put his right hand out. "Brent Brantley, U.S. Marshal."

Addison looked down at the extended hand, then back up into his face. "Sounds more like a character in one of those romance books the ladies in town are readin' than a name for a lawman."

Brantley pulled his hand back. Tate heard the man suck in a fast breath.

"We've tracked this man from California and aren't in the mood to take any shit from anyone, not even a lawyer. Now we can do this easy or hard, it's up to you." The lawman slapped his hat against his thigh, sending snow onto the floor in front of the desk. "Either way, we're gonna get satisfaction."

"Why don't you boys tell us what kind of satisfaction you're looking for? We got ourselves a nice little whorehouse, just the other side of the tracks. I'm sure Miss Addie's girls would scratch your itches and send you on your way outta town." He looked from one man to the other. "For a price, that is."

Tate struggled to keep a straight face, but it proved hard. Damn hard. He'd strapped on his gun belt before leaving home. Now he slid his right hand up under his jacket to rest it on his hip.

The lawyer had knocked the knees out from under the lawmen. Now they waited to see how long—or short—the marshal's fuse might be, and whether it'd been lit.

Boot heels tapped on the floor as the second fellow shifted behind the first. His face had gone beet red and his cheeks puffed out like a squirrel holding its winter nuts. But he hadn't said a word and it didn't look like he would. Brantley called the shots.

Addison didn't give either man a chance to speak. "Look, time's wastin' here. I'm sure Mister Taylor has better things to do than stand around. I know I do."

Brantley pulled his jacket back even further to reveal the star on his vest. "We have reason to believe Taylor is a fugitive from the law. He left California in possession of gold unlawfully gained from a claim he had no right to. We're here to take him back."

Addison glanced at Tate and raised an eyebrow.

"Well, can't say as we didn't expect this." The lawyer shrugged and when he did the seams on his shirt stretched so far the threads showed. "I assume this is about the Bodie gold."

Brantley gave a sharp nod. "It is. This man here took that gold from a claim he didn't own."

"Well, my client has paperwork that proves otherwise. And you can't rightly steal from yourself, now can you?" He crossed his arms over his chest and nodded toward the wall safe behind him. "Let's get this over with. Before one Abraham Calhoun died in Bodie, California, he signed his half of the jointly owned claim to his partner, one Tate Taylor. Despite gossip to the contrary and the claims of the decedent's sons, the old man stood in no way incapacitated and with a sound mind relinquished his hold on said claim."

Both men's faces reddened. The quiet one's cheeks grew so dark they were nearly purple.

Brantley sounded ready to brawl. "His sons have papers to the contrary."

The attorney rocked back and forth on his boot heels as a small grin played around the corners of his mouth.

"You'd best check those against Calhoun's signature. I've had the paperwork checked and authenticated. Mister Taylor and Mister Calhoun were business partners. When the old man grew ill he signed his half over to his partner and there ain't no law against that." The attorney placed his beefy hands on the desk and leaned forward. The scents of tobacco and peppermint wafted through the air. "We both know a man can't steal what he already owns. Any gold my client brought with him belongs to him. I'd say those two greedy boys done sent you both on a wild goose chase—in the middle of a snowstorm, no less."

The marshals looked at each other. The silent one shook his head as Brantley smacked his hat again. This time, it hit his leg hard, the noise almost a shot in the quiet room.

He gave it one more try. "I'd like to see those papers."

Addison nodded. "I'm sure you would. And I'll be happy to show them to you when you hand over a legal document stating I'm compelled to do so. Otherwise, I think you'd best head back out of town before word gets out that we got two marshals nosin' around and accusing innocent citizens of wrongdoing." He straightened up again, his full height making the marshals appear slight. With a slap of one large palm against his gun belt, he added, "We don't take kindly to that sort of thing in these parts."

Chapter 21

Tate didn't go straight home.

He watched the marshals head toward the Five Star Saloon, probably for a couple of shots to warm their bellies before their long ride back to gold rush territory.

He'd known the dead man's sons would give him trouble. They were a scurrilous pair, worthless and low-down, troublemakers for the old man from birth. It stood to reason they'd make waves for him, too, when Calhoun favored him over them.

Thank goodness for the paperwork the old miner insisted they sign. Without it, he'd be fighting to prove his ownership. He'd reached the point where he had no drive to fight anyone for anything. His whole life had been one tussle after another. Time to settle down, become a respectable business owner.

Find a wife.

Snow seeped down into the back of his jacket collar. He shook his head, hoping to send whatever accumulated on his shoulders flying off.

Damn, but when would this blasted storm end? It had been days without any sign of letting up. He looked to his left. Wylder Street had become a dirty snow-rutted lane. Horses managed it, but barely.

He turned Charles in the direction of the barn where freight had been stored following the derailment. Maybe he'd find the one missing carton there. If it didn't show up soon that meant it could be anywhere. Explosives in the wrong hands could prove deadly—and he didn't want to be responsible for any more deaths. His hands were already covered in the blood of dead men.

When he passed the schoolhouse, he saw all the footprints leading up to the door. They were small, mostly, and sunk deep in the snow. He stopped Charles beside the stone wishing well in front of the building and dismounted.

A shovel stood propped against the side of the building, so he grabbed it and got to work. Beneath the snow, an icy skim but by the time children departed it would be covered with a new layer of snow so there would be something for their boots to grip. He, however, slid along the slick patches more than once.

"What do you call that, the Wylder two-step?"

He looked up, brushed the snow from his brow, and frowned. What he didn't need, someone to witness his snowy clumsiness. And of course, it had to be Thomas Harvey. In a town filled with people why did the man have a habit of finding him in awkward positions?

One good jab sent the shovel into the snow far enough to lean an arm on it.

"Looking for a dance partner, Thomas?" Despite the stickiness of the situation, that the man probably surmised he'd left town because he'd lost Violet's heart, he strove for medium ground. He planned to put down roots in Wylder and it wouldn't do to have the mining financier think badly of him. "Although I hear you already have one, a pretty schoolteacher whose violet eyes could charm a snake."

The other man glanced toward the schoolhouse and smiled when the sounds of "Silent Night" came from the building.

"Sounds like Violet's got them practicing for the Christmas Eve party." He stared down at the ice at their feet before he met Tate's gaze. "But you're right, I am fortunate enough to have that wonderful woman on my arm. Have had for goin' on two years now."

The silence had to be filled, and he knew it, but what to say?

He'd learned to speak from the heart, the way southern gentlemen were taught from the earliest age. His lessons came from his grandfather, the man whose name he carried. Now, time to put what he'd been taught into practice and show his upbringing hadn't been neglected.

"I'm happy for you both. You seem like a good man, and she deserves that." He paused, then held out a hand. "Seems like the better man won the lady's heart."

The other took his gloved hand and gave it a good shake. Grandfather Taylor would like that the man shook like he meant it.

"I don't think that's the case. Violet thinks mighty highly of you. She's grateful you're here, not only in town but on this side of the dirt. From what she says it's a miracle you're alive. She cares for you." He paused to shrug. "But when two people meet sometimes there's a deep connection they make…and there's no battling with a heart, is there?"

He liked a man with integrity. Despite himself, Tate could see how a woman might find the guy interesting. And he had spoken the truth: What the heart wanted, it wanted. No denying it.

A relief that his own heart finally didn't yearn for the woman leading her charges in another off-key rendition of the holiday song.

"No battling it at all." He tapped a hand over his chest and sent snowflakes flying into the air between them. "God knows I tried for a long time. But I mean it, I'm glad you found each other. She deserves to be happy."

Harvey tipped his chin to his chest. "And I aim to keep her that way. I hope you find the same thing someday."

He mulled over his response before he opened his mouth. In the end, he let his heart talk again. "I think I have, actually."

"Well, that's great news. I hope you'll bring her to the Christmas party." He took a step toward the schoolhouse but stopped. A quick finger snap, soundless due to the black leather gloves on his hands. "Listen, I hear you have a mine out in California that's lying idle. Is that true or have the Wylder tongues been wagging out of turn?"

Small towns generate gossip. He knew it yet it unsettled him that he'd become part of the grapevine in a matter of weeks.

"It's the truth."

The financier clapped his hands together, then blew between them. Again, his gloves hampered his actions, but he didn't seem to mind. "I don't know if you're aware, but I have several mining interests. I'd like to talk with you about your mine. We both know a non-working parcel doesn't produce income. I think we might be able to remedy that, if you've a mind to listen to my ideas."

He had wondered what would come of the holdings he'd left behind. One man couldn't be in two places at the same time, and he wanted to settle in Wylder.

"I'd like to hear what you're thinking."

They both looked up at the snow that seemed determined to bury them.

The other man smiled. "Why don't we meet over lunch at the Five Star one day soon and talk it over? After the first of the year, when things settle down? We'll have the train wreck folks out of town by then, most likely. Wylder will be less busy so we won't be distracted. How does that sound?"

He pulled the shovel from the snow. "Sounds like a plan."

"Good."

They tipped their heads before the other man went toward the schoolhouse door. Tate finished clearing the walk, planted the shovel in the snow beside the wishing well, and mounted Charles.

As he turned toward Sidewinder Lane the man's words echoed in his head.

"We'll have the train wreck folks out of town..."

Chapter 22

"Are you positive this is a good idea? I mean, Tate will be back soon and I'm sure he wouldn't mind taking us to town." Meg gestured toward the building behind them. They'd hardly left it behind and she wished she'd stayed inside Tate's home. "It's not too late, we can turn back now."

She regretted letting herself be talked into this excursion the instant they stepped off the front walkway and her foot went down into snow nearly up to her knee. But Georgina had been insistent, and it proved impossible to deny the woman. After all, she'd nearly died—and had no qualms about bringing that up when it suited her purposes. How to refuse to accompany her on an outing after all she'd been through?

If Meg had more backbone she would've put the other woman off, but she didn't, so she slogged through snow in an unfamiliar town with someone she barely knew. And if matters weren't dicey enough, the day darkened by the minute. Had she been able to see the sun she would have watched it dip near the horizon but with the air filled with flakes that wouldn't happen.

Her companion dismissed her concerns. "Goodness, don't you have snow in Boston? We certainly have it in Chicago—and this is nothing compared to some of the storms we get there coming in off the lake."

She grabbed the other woman by the arm, forcing her to stop. "Chicago! Georgina, do you realize you remember where you're from? That's wonderful—what else about your past do you recall?"

They stared at each other for a long moment before the other woman shook her head.

Color drained from Georgina's lovely olive complexion. "I don't remember anything. And I probably got that detail from you when you tried to fill me in, that's all." Her dark gaze turned cold, all trace of friendliness gone. "Now, let's get moving so we have a chance to explore before the sun goes down."

The Reverend had taught Meg not to bear witness to liars. It pained her to think that her companion denied the truth, but she'd seen it in her eyes. Georgina recalled some of her past and the mention of Chicago storms proved it.

Not in the mood to argue, Meg trudged toward the railroad tracks. Tate's shop sat on the other side from town, behind a big building. Now she looked over at the place and wondered what it could be. Curtains hung at windows, the faint sound of a piano coming from beyond its windows gave it a homey air. Perhaps they were neighbors, a large family who needed lots of rooms.

She noticed a discreet little sign tucked in beside the door. Social Club. Now, wasn't that darling? An invitation to visit—and in a frontier town, no less.

She'd call on them in the next day or so. Maybe bring them an apple pie. Everyone in Wylder had been so accommodating she thought she should show some appreciation. Yes, a pie for the family beside Tate's business. Who could tell? Maybe they'd invite her inside for a slice and a cup of tea. She knew folks did things like that, although the Reverend never allowed it under his roof.

Well, she had escaped that roof. She could manage her own life now and act as she pleased. And she planned to do exactly that!

They crossed the tracks. Rumor had it that the train wreck hadn't been cleared yet so service from the east had come to an absolute standstill with the Union Pacific. They were to send crews out to the site when the weather broke but until then the line remained silent.

The train depot sat deserted. Hard to imagine that a few days ago they should have pulled into this station and may have even gotten off the train to stretch their legs. She wondered if she would have chosen to stay in town if they'd arrived as planned. With no destination in mind, she thought to linger in a place that seemed suitable for an unattached woman looking for employment.

Did Wylder have a house of ill repute? She had no idea but if it did she might have made a home here.

Now that could never happen. How could she become a soiled dove right under Tate's nose? She couldn't bear the thought of how he'd regard her if he witnessed her descent into that life. But her mother told her that women did whatever they had to do to survive. She had no other skills so the age-old profession would have to sustain her.

"Didn't Tate say people from the train are gathering in the saloon?" Georgina pointed to the building with a wide covered walkway in front of it and a sign that said Five Star Saloon hanging over its door.

"I hear music. Maybe they're having a party."

"Why would they do that on this snowy day? What's there to celebrate—we were in a train derailment, remember? Lots of people died."

"But we didn't. Being alive is reason to celebrate. Come on, let's see what's going on in there!" The other woman grabbed her hand and tugged her toward the walkway. They slipped once near the center of the lane, but they managed to make the front door without losing their footing.

She had never been inside a saloon and had no idea what lay beyond the swinging doors, but her friend didn't pause. Georgina pushed the wooden batwings wide and pulled her in behind her.

A saloon.

The Reverend would die if he knew. The devil sat on Meg's shoulder when she wished the horrid man were right here to witness her actions—and drop dead on the spot.

Chapter 23

Tate scowled when the two marshals walked through the door.

They had no business poking in the freight from the train so they must be sniffing around to see what he had up his sleeve. Well, they were wasting their time. He walked this side of the law and meant to keep it that way.

It didn't matter that they were here, anyway. His crate had not been recovered so he had nothing to show them—or to hide.

The men stood inside the door, so he paused near the exit to button his jacket.

"Don't you two have anything better to do than follow me around? I thought Merriweather made it clear that I didn't steal the claim."

Brantley shrugged. "Hey, we rode a long way. Gotta expect we're goin' to nose about a bit."

He shifted his gaze to the other marshal. It hit him that he hadn't heard the man utter a single syllable.

The urge to poke at the men who had come to take him in for a crime he hadn't committed sat heavy on his mind. He had a tolerant disposition, but any man might want a fair share of nonmonetary payback when it came to those who threatened his livelihood and peaceful life.

He met the quiet man's gaze. "So do you talk at all? Or are you just along for show?" He secured the last button and shook his head. "No need to answer. I can see you're not much on communicatin'—if you can even speak, that is."

A muscle worked near the man's jaw. Seeing it made Tate smirk. They should've stayed away, let him be. If they had, the man wouldn't be settin' to have a fit.

His Stetson in place, he headed for the door. He heard the wind howl and didn't relish the idea of going out in the mess, but he had no choice. Besides, Meg waited at home and that gave him incentive to hurry.

But he couldn't resist one last jab.

"Well, nice seein' you guys again. Hope the storm don't bite you in the ass on that long, cold ride back to Bodie." He glanced at the silent marshal, then met Brantley's gaze. He tipped his head to the quiet man. "Hell, at least that one won't give you a headache, jabbering all day long. Good work, taking on a partner who's too dumb to talk."

The marshal let out a growl and pulled his right arm back. Brantley reached to grab him but didn't move quickly enough. The man swung at Tate but years of boxing with his cousins taught him well. He ducked and the fist intended for his jaw met with the solid wood door instead.

"You sonofabitch!" The man grabbed his hand, cradled it to his chest, and spit. Blood spilled from his knuckles. "You broke my hand, damnit!"

Brantley smacked his hat against his thigh and swore.

Tate shook his head. "Good to see you can speak, after all. But hell, I didn't jump a claim and I didn't break any part of you. It wouldn't hurt you any to reconsider how you see things. Might save you some travel—and it'd sure save your hands."

Chapter 24

It took all of ten minutes for Meg to decide the Reverend had been right about one thing: Saloons were no place for a refined woman. All around her, whiskey sloshed from glasses, loud laughter filled the air, and the haze of tobacco smoke hung heavy in the room.

To one side a few tables were occupied by those who looked like travelers, but every other spot held revelers intent on having a good time. She heard more than one toast to "the Christmas storm!" and from near the door came the request for whiskey shots to commemorate surviving the derailment.

"Georgina, we should get out of here." She leaned close to speak into the other woman's ear, so she'd be heard above the din. "Everyone is intoxicated. I think we should get back to Tate's."

Her train mate had appeared refined, markedly different from the woman who flirted with a man standing on her other side. She did not turn when she answered from the corner of her mouth, keeping a smile in place for the grizzled one who set a glass in front of her. "We're having fun, aren't we? What's the harm in that?"

She guessed the glass held beer but never having touched a drop of alcohol couldn't be sure. Another cheer, more downed shots, and exclamations about surviving filled the air again.

"This is not fun."

Her companion swallowed a healthy portion of her beverage, then let out a small burp along with a giggle hidden behind her hand. It looked as if she and the brew were well acquainted. Meg wondered how she could have misjudged the other's character so completely. How could a woman—well-read, worldly, and graceful—turn into a common saloon girl in a heartbeat? It didn't make sense, both that Georgina behaved so badly but also that she had been thoroughly fooled by her.

"Don't be such a wet rag." Her friend held her refilled glass beneath Meg's nose. "Here, try this. It'll loosen you up."

The smell of unwashed bodies mixed with the sweet scent of sugar, yeast, and something she couldn't identify swept up her nose. The thickness of it turned her stomach so she raised a hand to push it away, sending it sloshing over onto the sticky floor.

"No, please. I don't want any of that." She ran a finger under her nose and met her friend's glare with a frown. "I mean it. I want to leave."

The man buying drinks reached around and waved her away. "Then go home! No need to put a cloud on the party. Hell, I rode in from Cheyenne, freezing my balls off. I saw enough damn clouds and I'm ready for some fun so if you're not, head out. The door's over yonder."

The wiry whiskered cowboy looked like he'd rolled in soot but when he turned back and swept a kiss over her friend's cheek it did not bring any objection. His actions did send her gut lurching again, so she leaned close to Georgina and hollered, "I'm going home."

The other woman met her gaze with eyes that were already glazed. She nodded and offered a tiny smile, but Meg's patience had fled.

She turned toward the door. A solid wall of male chest stopped her.

The man stood average height with a broad torso and ample girth. His brown jacket, stained in spots, stretched over his arms and did not close in front. A mix of body odor and horseflesh wafted off him.

Tilting her head back until she met his gaze, she swallowed her irritation and mustered her own grin. If getting out of the Five Star in one piece and finding her way back to Tate's unharmed meant she had to smile at stinky men, so be it.

"Excuse me, please." She tipped her head to the space beside him. "I'd like to get by."

His face split into a wide grin, showing several missing teeth and brown spots on those that remained. The sight did little to calm her already queasy gut, so she looked into his eyes, determined to not vomit on her own feet.

"Well, lookee here. A fancy lady in Wylder. You must be from the train, am I right?"

She nodded.

"Well, we need to show some hospitality. Let me buy you a drink. How 'bout some whiskey to take the chill off them delicate bones of yours?" He didn't wait for her to respond before snapping his fingers at the barkeep. "Two whiskeys, Stan."

"No, thank you. I don't want anything to drink. I just want to get out of here." She considered pushing past but doubted her strength capable to shift his position. His form did not look muscular but fleshy—and immovable. "Please, let me get past."

"Not so fast. We haven't even introduced ourselves yet." He reached for the first shot and downed it. When he leaned over to put the glass on the bar he brushed against her with a leer that told her it had been no accident.

Disgust strengthened her. She prepared to jab an elbow in his side but before she landed it, a hand claimed hers. Its owner, dressed in a saloon girls' low-cut bodice and high-waisted, flouncy skirt, leaned against the man.

"Come on, Rob, leave the lady alone." She gave him another shove and opened up enough room to pull Meg past him. "Save your shenanigans for those who get paid to put up with you."

From behind she heard the man object, but her new friend didn't hesitate. They moved quickly through the crowd and stopped near the door.

She got a good look at her rescuer then. Rouge covered creamy cheeks, black lined stunning green eyes, and had her hair not been teased to an outrageous height it might have flowed in auburn waves down her slender back.

"Thank you." A deep breath calmed her racing pulse. She had been frightened yet hadn't realized it until this very moment.

A smile. "Glad I saw Rob bothering you. Believe me, you don't want to squander your time with him." The saloon girl twittered, then held up her hand. She brought her thumb and index fingers about two inches apart. "Man worked for the post office but got fired a while back. The only thing smaller than his brain is his pecker."

Despite her hurry to leave, she giggled. "He sounds horrible."

The other woman nodded. "Oh, he is. The only good part of servicing him is he's fast on the draw. Over before you know it!" She motioned toward the doorway. "Now get on out of here before I have to rescue you from another creep. Careful, though, the snow's thicker than Santa's beard out there."

Chapter 25

Tate didn't feel one ounce of remorse over the marshal's hand.

He did, however, regret not finding his property. That it had not shown up, all these days later, could only mean one of two things. Either it had been buried by snow at the crash site and would surface in the spring thaw, or someone else had the goods.

It crossed his mind to stop in to see the sheriff who had replaced the old guy, Hanson, but why fritter away time? Whether buried beneath snow or tucked in someone's barn, whatever harm the explosives might do could not be dumped on his shoulders. Time to cut his losses and forget about it. There were more pressing matters to claim his attention—like his enchanting houseguest.

His upturned collar did not keep snow from finding its way down the back of his jacket. An icy finger dampened his hair, leaving another inch of him open to freezing. Well, he only had this and one more stop before he could head home. An extra bit of body ice wouldn't matter much.

Charles kept his head down when they stopped in front of the mercantile. He slid off the horse's back and took the snowy steps two at a time. He'd been too long from home. Time didn't usually matter but then he didn't ordinarily have a woman waiting on him, either.

Finn Wylder stood behind the counter, towering over others like a tall maple surrounded by saplings. A pleasant man, with light brown hair and gentle brown eyes, he treated every customer as if they were family.

Now he looked up from the shelf he'd been stocking. "Howdy, Tate. Good to see you back in town." He placed a box of talcum powder beside others and straightened the row before turning away. "Christmastime, you know. So hard to keep the shelves full, especially this year with so many extra folks in town. Tragic, the derailment, but good, too, that so many were saved."

Tate crossed the floor and stopped beside the sweets display. Every woman had a sweet tooth, didn't they?

"Two sides to a coin, it seems. Good and bad, all in one." The pickings were getting slim, a testament to the number of stockings to be filled before the week ended. His gaze fell on the mints, so he pointed. "I'll take two bags of those, please. And if you could tie 'em up with ribbons, that'd be mighty fine."

The shop owner scooped red-and-white candies into two white paper sacks. He used two lengths of dark green ribbon to add bows before he slid them across the counter. Tate placed coins down and tucked the bags into his jacket pocket.

The other man slid the coins back. "Heard how you were the first on the scene, how you checked the engineer with the bloodied face before jumping into a burning car to pull people out. No charge for a hero. Candy's on me."

A lump formed in his throat as he brushed Finn's words aside. "We were all there, the whole town, practically."

"I heard. Branch, he's the sheriff now, well he's been saying you showed up before he did, even."

That made sense. The man who treated him as if he'd had no intellect—a lawman trying to secure a scene.

Branch Wylder. One of Finn's kinfolk, then.

"I saw him that night."

"Well, he saw you, too. And I hear you got a couple of ladies staying with you, that you scooped 'em right outta the burning train and took 'em home." He crossed his arms over his chest and lowered his voice. "Saw 'em with you a day or so ago. Didn't say anything 'cause I didn't want to make them feel uncomfortable, if you get my meaning."

Tate nodded. Even in a week-long snowstorm, tongues flapped, and news spread as fast as grease through a goose. He didn't bother to deny it, only smiled and shrugged. "What else could a man do but help damsels in distress? Any of us would've done the same thing."

He turned toward the door, but Finn tapped the counter beside the money with an insistent finger. "Don't insult me, now. Please, take this and buy yourself a shot or two. Or better yet, take one of those ladies out for dinner at the hotel. Seems you should get some kindness for putting your life on the line."

He slid the coins off the edge of the counter and into his palm with a soft whisper. "Appreciate it, Finn."

The other man brushed aside his thanks with a quick nod.

"We're glad you're back in town. Hear you're opening a mining supply over behind the Social Club."

He tipped the brim of his hat back on his head. "Doesn't anything get past you? You have the pulse of the whole town, don't you?"

The shop owner lifted his shoulders, then let them fall. "What can I say? I hear a lot—and believe me, there's a ton of stuff that hits these ears that I wish I'd never heard." He chuckled. "But seriously, good luck with the business. I can't keep much in the way of miner's gear here and to be honest I don't know a lick about mining, so you're doing the town a service. Let me know if I can help in any way."

"That's mighty kind of you."

"Hey, we gotta stick together. It's the only way Wylder's gonna grow." He pointed to the scene outside the wide front window. "Now you'd best be gettin' home. It's still ugly out there—helluva week, huh?"

Tate nodded a goodbye and then pulled his collar tighter before he headed for the door. Yes, it'd been one hell of a week—but not all bad to his way of thinking.

Chapter 26

Her fingers and toes could be missing for all she could tell. And one road looked the same as the next with snow whipping through the air.

The big house she used as a reference point did not appear where she thought it should, so she kept her head down and plodded through the blizzard.

Ahead, the sound of men's laughter. She raised her chin and peered into the swirling flakes. A square of light appeared out of the darkness, so she put one foot in front of the other and went toward it.

A church. She'd seen it when Tate took them to claim their bags. Now she could not recall where it sat in relation to his place.

The Reverend's voice invaded her mind. *"Women aren't smart enough to find their way out of a cloth sack."*

She shoved him from her head and turned left, toward the voices carrying on the wind. Cloth sack be damned. She'd found her way this far and she'd damn well make it farther.

Heat shot through her veins and fueled by anger she yanked at the frozen scarf wound around her neck. Pulling it higher on her cheeks only made her skin wetter but at least it saved her from the icy pinpricks pelting her.

Anger made her careless. Clumsy, too. She

stumbled over her feet and fell forward onto her knees. Her arms dug elbow deep in snow which made finding a spot to steady herself impossible. Pushing down only dropped her closer to the freezing mess but she shoved one arm in as far as she could and tried to lift herself.

Her face went down in one heart-stopping sweep. Her knees slid and her skirt rose onto her thighs as she lay prone on the deserted street.

At least no one witnessed her indelicate position but if she didn't figure out how to find her feet—and soon—she had no doubt she'd freeze to death.

Meg kicked at the snow and twisted onto her side. Her skirt swathed her legs as thickly as a mummy's wrappings. A groan escaped her as she jerked from side to side looking for a firm spot to push against.

Anger turned to despair. Perhaps the Reverend had been right all these years. Maybe she served no good purpose on this earth. Dying in a snowstorm might show others something useful. She couldn't imagine what but if she served as an example of how not to misuse a life that would be something, anyway.

Hell's bells, whatever was she thinking? She might die trying to save herself, but she'd come too far to lie down and give up. And she'd rather kiss Satan himself than give the Reverend one ounce of satisfaction over having been right about her. The old bastard hadn't known her, or her mother, and if it took every bit of strength to prove that—even if only to herself—that's what she'd do.

She shoved her left hand into the snow right up to her armpit, and pressed down. She made it back onto her knees and rested a minute. Fat flakes landed on her head and flew past her nose.

The sound of a horse's breathing carried on the thick, wintry air caught her attention. She peered into the night, hoping that whoever rode the animal would stop to help. When it grew closer, she sat back on her heels and waved her arms. They felt made of wood, so stiff and cold she could hardly feel them.

"H-help! P-please, help!" Her teeth chattered so hard she wondered if they'd crack. "H-h-help!"

The horse pulled up and a man jumped off its back. He crossed the distance in a couple of long strides, reached down, and lifted her to her feet. When her knees buckled, he put an arm beneath them and brought her into his arms.

"Meg! What the hell are you doing in the storm? Don't you realize you could die out here?" Tate carried her to his horse and, holding her against his chest, climbed into the saddle. "I don't know what's gotten into people tonight. Those two fools over at the wishing well, making wishes like schoolgirls in the middle of a raging snowstorm. Now you, half frozen kneeling in front of the church like it's Sunday morning and you're waiting on the preacher."

He smelled comfortingly familiar when she buried her face against his neck and melted into him. The soothing rhythm of the horse laid the fear building inside her to rest and she breathed a long, soft sigh. He'd opened his coat and nestled her body to his, and the heat of the man seeped into her.

She didn't know how she'd been given the gift of knowing such a man, but gratitude flooded her heart and soul. It might be only a short association and she knew that what waited her would never be as beautiful as this. But if these short days were the only loving ones she'd know in her lifetime, she'd be eternally thankful that train crashed on this man's doorstep.

Chapter 27

Tate kicked the back door open and rushed through to the front room. Embers glowed in the hearth, so he put the half-frozen woman in a chair and set to work bringing the fire to life. A few well-placed bits of kindling and some steady streams of air and it burst into flames. He adjusted the draft before he went into the kitchen to kindle the one there, too.

When both cookstove and fireplace were roaring, he returned to Meg. She hadn't moved, which worried him some.

Her blue-tinged lips dropped his heart to his boot tips.

"Come on, let's get these wet things off you." He unwrapped her scarf, peeled away her gloves, and went for the buttons on her coat. Her body shook and she gave him a glazed stare as he undid her boots and slipped them from her feet. Stockings came next. Without the fabric to hide the truth, he saw her toes were blue, too.

Hell, he sat on the verge of losing the one person who mattered most to him. He wouldn't let it happen— not if he had to wrap her with his own body until she came back to him.

He'd put pots of water on the stove to warm and dragged the tub into the center of the kitchen floor. By the time he got her undressed they should be ready—or so he hoped.

No time for gentle meandering. He tugged at the buttons on her shirtwaist. When one popped off and flew across the room he didn't care. Her upper body exposed, he grabbed a blanket from the back of the chair and wrapped her in it before he stood her up and unbuttoned her skirt. It fell in a puddle at her feet. Undergarments followed.

He took her in his arms and ran for the kitchen, where both heat sources had done a fine job of warming the room. A toe tucked behind a leg let him drag a chair close to the fire. He set her down and turned to the pots.

He dumped the water in the tub before refilling the pots and settling them back on the stove. The water level hit the halfway mark, so he carried Meg over and set her in the water, blanket and all.

She shivered, then gasped as heat touched her skin. With one hand he supported her back when she seemed too stiff to lie against the metal surface. The other hand brought streams of water up to drizzle over her. A little river down her neck, another wave of droplets across her shoulders, more splashed up on her belly.

The shaking continued.

"Meg, honey can you hear me?" His heart hammered in his chest when she stared at him. God, but he couldn't lose her now! "I know you're cold, but do you understand what's happening? Do you know who I am?"

She nodded. A twitch of the lips may have been an effort to smile, he couldn't tell for sure although he hoped so.

This wouldn't do. She couldn't warm up quickly enough.

No time to fetch the doctor. In this storm, she'd die before he got back with Coyote.

The water in the second round of pots simmered so he added it to the bath.

Then he stood and removed his clothes.

He eased his body into the tub behind hers, slipped the blanket out of the way, and wrapped his arms around her. The wet blanket draped over the bottom edge of the tub, forming a tent that kept the steam rising off the water swirling around their legs.

"It's gonna be all right, I promise. Stay with me, honey." Water lapped at their skin in slow, gentle waves. He swished a foot over her toes, massaging them with his own. At first she didn't respond but finally he felt one toe wiggle. Then, the others.

"That's right. It might pain you a little when the feeling comes back into those frozen parts, but we'll get through it." He swished water up over her arms, to her shoulders. His fingertips massaged the skin as they moved back down toward the surface. He spoke softly, as he would to a spooked horse, and waited for her to recover.

Murmuring. Sweeping water, dribbling it over skin that began to turn pink. Gentle movements.

Love.

That he loved her hadn't escaped his mind or heart.

He'd known it almost the minute he pulled her from the train when she'd struggled to return to save her companion. That she would jeopardize her own life for the sake of another showed the essence of the woman.

Every moment they'd spent together deepened his feelings.

Now he wanted to swap places with her, offer up his comfort to restore hers.

She still shook, but it diminished. The water remained warm, heated by the temperature of the air around them as well as the blanket still tented over the tub.

In slow, soft stages she settled back against him, thawing into him so he didn't need to pull her close. Her skin took on a healthy glow and her breathing came naturally. No more gasps or tortured wheezes, just an ease to show her lungs warmed up.

Good. Heating her insides meant as much as defrosting the exterior parts.

He'd seen men die from the cold, not recover from their internal chill to the point that it took their lives. He'd feared the fate for Meg, but this softening gave him hope.

Her hair curled as it dried. Gold strands glistened in the firelight.

He leaned in close, placed his cheek against her head, and did something he didn't ordinarily do: Tate prayed. He and God hadn't ever had much of a relationship, despite his Grandfather Taylor's best efforts. But he vowed that if the man in the sky let Meg regain her strength after this, he'd surely begin attending church on a regular basis.

He'd do anything to keep her here.

"Hmm…" She wiggled her bottom against him, wrapped her arms around his where they circled her, and sighed. "I…"

"Save your strength. We can talk later."

Their fingers twined together, and she settled more firmly against him. They fit together so well it felt as if she'd been made precisely to join his angles and planes with her soft curves. He knew now what had always been missing from his life and never wanted to be without it again. Never.

Chapter 28

Meg lay back in Tate's bed.

He'd insisted on carrying her upstairs despite her protest that she could walk.

She wore one of his flannel shirts and a pair of his thick socks. He'd added an extra quilt, tucked her in, and asked that she remain in place until his return.

The fire roared and heat suffused the room.

Cold no longer invaded her body or clouded her mind.

Waiting had never been this difficult. But she'd given her word and would keep it, even if every inch of her wanted to run downstairs and leap into the man's arms. Her body lay in his bed, but her heart sat in his hands.

What would he do if he knew she loved him?

She couldn't tell him. In a few days she'd be gone, on a stagecoach to Laramie. Maybe farther now that she knew Tate. The possibility he might stumble upon her one evening in a madam's parlor made her blood run cold. That couldn't happen so as much as she wished to stay close to him, she'd have to go all the way to California.

The bedroom door opened so she left off musing about the future. What mattered stood right in front of her holding a tray laden with bowls that smelled so delicious saliva pooled on her tongue.

"Let's get some food into you." He placed the tray on the bedside table. A kitchen towel draped across his shoulder. He laid it over the blankets covering her lap and sat down on the edge of the bed.

When he lifted a spoon and dipped it into one of the bowls, she saw what he meant to do and held up a hand.

"No, Tate. You don't have to trouble yourself." The spoonful of soup hung in the air. "I can feed myself."

He tilted his head and pulled his brows together. "Are you sure? I don't mind."

"I am. And I see you've got a bowl for you, too, so why don't you climb in next to me? That way we can eat together." She felt heat rise on her cheeks when she nodded toward his bare chest. "You don't want to get chilled out there, do you?"

Glancing down, he shook his head with a grin. "You've got a mighty fine point."

She took the bowl and spoon he offered, then watched him go around the bottom of the bed to the other side. He wore blue jean trousers held closed on his hips by only two buttons. The rest were undone, a reminder of what he barely covered.

If she kept thinking like this her body might combust and forget it had ever been frozen!

Tate climbed into bed beside her and they both settled back against the pillows propped before the plain pine headboard. A knot on a log popped in the fireplace, the only sound aside from their breathing and swallowing for several long minutes.

She hadn't known her body needed sustenance so badly. The soup disappeared without any trouble—and she hadn't believed herself at all hungry.

He took both bowls and spoons and placed them on the table beside him.

"Should I get some more? There's a whole pot down in the kitchen."

Placing a hand on her belly she shook her head. "No, thanks. I'm quite satisfied."

Shadows danced in the corners. The scent of hickory perfumed the air. The candle on the mantel flickered, sending a fuzzy kaleidoscope of dancing lights onto the ceiling.

Tate placed a palm on her face and ran his thumb down the center of her nose. Their gazes locked. "Your beautiful face is finally warm. You scared me, you know."

"I scared me, too." She pressed into his hand. The feel of him warmed even the faintest corners of her body. "If you hadn't come along—"

He covered her lips with a tender fingertip. "Don't, please. I can't stand to think of it." He dipped his face close and touched his forehead to hers. She felt his breath, warm and smelling faintly of soup, touch her skin. "My heart about stops every time I…no, I can't let it into my head. The sight of you in the snow…"

Her turn to silence him so she brought her lips over his and kissed him. His mouth had grown familiar, and every ounce of shyness had fled days ago. Her hand went to the side of his neck and angled his chin. His tongue swept across her lower lip, sending still more heat running along her skin and deeper, into her center.

The shirt slipped off her shoulder. His lips trailed a line down the side of her neck and across the exposed skin as she dropped her hand to his chest. She rested it in the center, above his heart, and felt the beat that matched her own.

How had she lived this long without realizing her heart had a twin?

His voice rumbled in his chest. "I'm not sure we should be doing this, honey. The doc would probably have my hide for exciting you after what happened."

"The doctor isn't here. And no one is going to have any part of you tonight..." She kissed his neck, then gave it a tiny nip before lifting her head and meeting his gaze. "Except me, that is. And I plan to have every part at least once."

He grinned and shook his head so hard the brown hair she favored so much swept across his shoulder. Her fingers found a home in its softness as they stared into each other's eyes.

"I know you were...well, that you hadn't known a man before you met me." He paused and ran a gentle hand down her arm until he reached her hand. He took it and gave it a small squeeze. "I am honored that I'm the man you chose, although had I known I would have made it much more special, if you know what I mean. I would have—"

She hated that he believed any of their first lovemaking had been anything but a dream come true. More than that, really, since she'd never allowed herself to entertain the notion that such a good, kind, generous man would ever want to share a bed with her.

"I wouldn't have had it any other way, Tate. My first time was perfect, I promise."

He gave a satisfied nod. She wouldn't want him to think that she regretted anything they'd done or how he'd loved her. These nine days had been more than she believed possible between a man and woman.

Her only regret? That it would end.

"I'm relieved to hear that because I've been wondering." He cleared his throat. "There's something else that's on my mind."

Uh oh.

Meg mustered her courage and took a deep breath. Time to face whatever had put the serious expression on his handsome face.

"What's that?"

His brilliant blue eyes held hers as if they were connected by an invisible thread. She could drown in the man's gaze and be swept away by him.

"Why did you choose me? You'd saved yourself, yet you came to this room that night and made it clear that you were ready and willing. How did I get so lucky?"

Her whole life had been one big lie. That the Reverend kept a home filled with love. That she and her mother were happy and treated well. Running from Boston had been a lie, too. She'd pretended to be someone she wasn't heading to an unknown place—where she planned to pretend to be comfortable doing something she'd never done.

If she lived through one moment of truth in her life, this had to be it—with the only person who showed her unconditional love and never let her down.

She might lose him, but her leaving grew closer and she would lose him then, anyhow.

Better to live the truth for a moment than a lie forever.

Meg took a deep breath, then released it on a long, slow sigh. "I told you about the Reverend. Not a good man, he hurt Mother and me. Physically and emotionally, he beat us down. And he said women were only good for one thing."

When Tate tried to pull her close she put a hand on his chest and pushed him back so she could meet his gaze. A fast shake of her head when he opened his mouth. She'd come this far—she had to finish.

"Mother agreed that women were born to service men's needs and since I've no other skills…" She swallowed hard. "I decided to gain employment in a house of ill repute. But first, I needed to know how it felt for real, when there's some intimacy…when it's not for money."

His eyes became stormy. Their Atlantic Ocean depths showed crashing waves, so she waited. Whatever he had to say, she deserved. If he threw her out now, she would hate it but would go. A man of morals, he probably despised her.

He reached behind him and opened the bed table drawer. When he turned back, he held a small box. It had a periwinkle blue ribbon tied in a bow around it.

"I'm sorry you haven't been shown how precious you are, Meg. It rips my heart to pieces to hear that you believe you're worth so little when I hold you in such high regard."

Her ears played tricks on her! How could he feel that way after all she'd admitted?

"You must think me deplorable now. I told you what I mean to do, Tate. How can you even bear the sight of me?" She tugged her hand, trying to pull it from his grasp but he didn't release her. "I should go—"

He closed the space between them and put his mouth on hers. A lingering, tender kiss.

When he pulled back his gaze held hers. "If you go, I will follow you. Through any storm, over mountains and deserts—I will stay on your trail. I can't bear the thought of you leaving me." He held her cheek in his hand and rubbed her temple with his thumb. "Don't you see how much I love you?"

Her heart grew so warm it felt as if it would burst from her chest.

His gaze said all the things that were in her own mind and heart, and much more. She saw so many emotions written on his face that her throat tightened. She'd experienced such little sentiment in her life that this overwhelmed her.

Her voice came out as a whisper. "I didn't know how it felt to love someone...until you." A tear slid down her cheek, but she didn't care. "Thinking about leaving you is killing me."

His thumb caught the tear. "You're not going anywhere, honey. We belong together." Tate pressed the box into her hand. "I thought to give this to you tomorrow, but I think this is a better time."

She untied the bow and laid the ribbon to the side. Her fingers shook, from emotion rather than cold or fear, but she managed to lift the lid. Her breath caught. A necklace, the only one she'd ever been given.

Tate lifted the delicate gold chain and held it up. She swept her hair off her shoulders so he could fasten it around her neck. It hung nearly to the slope of her breasts and nestled against her skin like his thumbprint on her heart.

"It's beautiful." The hand she covered the pendant with shook. "I don't know what to say. Thank you isn't nearly enough."

He kissed her. "It's more than enough." He covered her hand with his, then spread her fingers so he could touch the stone where it lay on her skin. "It's blue topaz, from California. I mined it myself and a man in town made it into the necklace."

"You found the stone?" When she believed he couldn't shock her again he proved her wrong. "As in you pulled it from the earth?"

He grinned. "Something like that. I love you, Meg. Merry Christmas a little bit early."

She melted into his arms and wrapped herself around him. It occurred to her that suddenly the room felt hot, and she had too many clothes on. Tate, too.

Time to show the man how much feeling went behind the words she murmured against his cheek. "I love you, too…"

Chapter 29

Christmas Eve morning came with beautiful surprises.

Meg woke next to Tate, naked except for the blue topaz necklace. She rolled over and kissed him awake.

"Good morning." He looked over her shoulder toward the window. "Is that blue sky I see?"

"Storm's over, I think." She rested against him and twined her fingers into his. "I thought it'd never end." She'd hoped it would go on forever so she could remain right here. Now she planned to stay, even if Wylder never saw another snowflake.

He cleared his throat and pointed one finger to the bedside table. A folded piece of paper propped against the box that had held the necklace.

"That note is from Georgina. I found it on the kitchen table when I went down during the night to check the fireplace. Seems she isn't who she led you to believe. I'm sorry, honey."

A quick turn to her side put them nearly face to face again. Whatever the note said, she'd rather see him than a scrap of paper.

"What did she say?"

He shrugged, sending his muscles rippling and distracting her for a second. My, but the man's body simmered her blood!

"Her memory returned almost as soon as she woke

after the derailment, but she said she needed time to think so she pretended not to remember anything." His tone showed compassion. "I guess we all have things we don't want to find us or times we'd rather forget. For Georgina, it's a husband who treats her badly back in Chicago. A cousin who offered her a place to hide until she sorts her life out. And a man from the frontier who she met in the Five Star and decided to go away with."

Well, if that didn't beat all!

"I thought I had a closet full of secrets but mine are no match for hers." She thought for a moment, then met his gaze. "Do you think she'll be safe with the man from the saloon? He seemed to care for her, but I don't know in what way, if you know what I mean."

Another shrug and a second wave of simmering in her veins.

"If she were a young, inexperienced woman I'd be more concerned. But she's married from a big city. I'm bettin' she can take care of herself." He dropped a fast kiss on her lips. "And there's a wad of cash on the table downstairs. A thick bundle of currency and some silver. The note says her husband is as wealthy as he is nasty and won't miss the money. She wants you to have it, to begin your new life, she says."

The world tilted.

Suddenly she had more than she'd even dreamed possible.

Added to the meager funds tucked in her mother's old reticule, she could now, for the first time ever, feel financially secure. Depending on the generosity of others taught one to have faith in the world to provide but being able to care for oneself brought a measure of peace. She'd longed for that feeling her whole life, and now it belonged to her.

The profession she dreaded but accepted as her lot in life would not claim her. She need never know the touch of a man she did not love. And realizing her worth as more than a man's plaything bestowed dignity she'd not experienced.

She did not need to worry about homelessness. Wandering aimlessly on unfamiliar streets or bedding down in a dirty alley had been nightmares plaguing her. Now she could banish them from her darkest hours. Sleep would no longer be an elusive bedfellow. She would rest easy.

In Tate's arms.

That she had gone from being entirely alone and fleeing Boston to finding love in Wylder almost sent her mind off its rails the way the train had gone flying. But she took a deep breath and snugged her body up against the man who held her as if she were a priceless jewel.

"Is that a sigh of contentment? Or hunger?" He chuckled when her belly rumbled. "That's what I thought. We've slept in, haven't we? The perfect way to begin Christmas Eve."

She wiggled closer and felt his response to her nearness—which sent heat thrumming along her body. That he could make her feel so much without touching her filled her with joy. And the way he touched her…well, that affected her in a way she doubted she'd ever take for granted.

His love was pure magic.

His chest rumbled beneath the cheek where she lay listening to his heartbeat.

"Hmm…if you keep movin' like that we may have to delay breakfast." He ran a hand over her back, letting it drift lower than her waist.

Meg kissed the spot where his heart beat and squirmed a bit more. And, as she knew he would, he reacted with increased vigor.

She smiled as she raised her face to his. "I'm thinking we might satisfy our appetites here before we head down to the kitchen—unless you're hungrier for eggs and bacon than you are for me." With newly discovered confidence she raised an eyebrow in what she hoped showed a sensual intent.

His arms wrapped around her when he brought his lips to hers. "I will never be hungrier for anything on that kitchen table than I am for you." He teased her mouth open and kissed her so thoroughly she forgot about anything but the feel of his touch. With a growl, he pulled back for an instant. "Unless it's you on the table, that is."

Chapter 30

Christmas Eve afternoon Tate suggested a buggy ride around town. They had a while before the party at the schoolhouse and now that the snow stopped, he wanted her to see more of Wylder.

And he wanted Wylder to see more of her. He had never been a pretentious man, but Meg deserved to be shown off. Her life until this point had been dismal and filled with cruelty, and she'd never felt valued or loved. He planned to show her how much she meant to him. He would walk the streets of Wylder with the prettiest woman in town on his arm—until she realized her own self-worth. And then, he'd spend the rest of his days walking through life with her on his arm, knowing he'd been blessed with an angel on earth.

His heart swelled every time he gazed at the woman. Her arrival in his life caught him wholly off guard but he loved that she appeared like a gift from above in the worst snowstorm he'd experienced. And riding a train to its final destination, besides.

She showed him that his plan hadn't been enough to sustain a man for life. A new start in a place with lots of down-to-earth, kind folks began things off on a good foot but left a big hole—right in his heart, where it mattered most. Meg filled that spot so completely he began to forget how lonely he'd been without her.

Today she wore one of the fancy dresses that hung

in the wardrobe that came with the building. The last owner's wife never got to wear the items stored there which saddened him. But seeing them put to good use on his beautiful lady replaced those somber feelings with light.

She chose a dress that matched her eyes. The palest periwinkle blue, its fitted bodice hugged every curve and accentuated her tiny waistline. The neckline scooped low enough that the necklace nestled between her breasts for all to see. He watched Meg touch it more than once, a quick fingertip rubbed across its polished face. It felt as if she swiped her skin over his own heart, too, when she did that.

He doubted any man could be happier on this glorious day.

When he'd mined the gem he recognized its value, but he'd never imagined he would ever find a woman who wore it the way Meg did. It looked made to nestle against her skin, as if the earth had known the gentle slope of her bosom existed and created something special just for her to wear.

They walked down Wylder Street a way, her arm tucked into his and her body as near as possible without causing gossip.

Most shop owners shoveled paths in front of their buildings so foot traffic could pass with ease. They had nothing to buy so they simply meandered. Sunshine after snow almost demanded they get out. And it looked as if the rest of the town's residents felt the same way. The boardwalks were filled with foot traffic and wagon wheels made a shushing sound as they cut through snow.

Every few feet, someone greeted him. The warm

welcome back to town lifted his spirits even higher than they already were.

"Tate, it's good to see you! I heard you were back but with the weather bein' so nasty I haven't had a chance to swing by." Theo Harvey shook his hand. Then he tipped his hat to Meg. "And I heard from the ladies that you'd met someone nice. They didn't warn me she's so pretty, though."

He didn't take offense. Thomas' brother lived on a homestead and while he had some rough edges, he had a good heart, so he made introductions. He'd married Violet's eldest sister, Lily. They had one son and another child on the way.

"Nice to meet you, Mister Harvey."

"The pleasure's all mine. Will I see you two at the party later on?"

Harvey looked to him for a reply but the sweet woman on his arm answered for them.

"We're looking forward to it."

He nodded to the other man and continued walking. It pleased him that she fell so naturally into acknowledging them as a couple. After the life she'd led it wouldn't have surprised him if she shied away from folks. No one, especially not him, would blame her if that were the case. But the lady stepped right up with Harvey, and that gave him hope that she'd feel at home in town sooner rather than later.

They crossed the street. Liu Wei's gemstone shop might interest her. If she seemed attracted to something, he'd give the merchant a nod to hold it for him. His gold didn't bring joy sitting in the bank vault. He'd love the opportunity to spoil her.

He hadn't told her yet about his wealth. There

would be time enough later to explain about the Bodie gold. He had more money than a man could spend in a lifetime, but he already hoped they would have children he could leave it to when he passed.

But he got ahead of himself. Better to enjoy the day. The future would take care of itself.

The merchant welcomed them into his place of business. He hailed from China, a man of medium height with a slender build. His long black hair hung down his back.

"Meg, Mister Liu made your necklace. I brought the gemstone to him, and he worked his artistry with it."

Her gloved fingertips went to the jewel. She'd refused to close her coat all the way to the top and while she insisted she didn't want to be too warm he suspected the pleasure of displaying the gift motivated her.

"Thank you for making the necklace. I love it." Her fingers danced over the skin near where it hung. "It's stunning."

The Chinese man nodded. His hands clasped near his waist, sending the wide sleeves on his deep blue jacket hanging like twin sails. When he spoke, his accent turned his words almost poetic.

"That is a beautiful stone. Not as pretty as its owner but still, it has special significance."

Meg gasped. "What do you mean?"

The man smiled. His eyes, so dark as to be nearly black, glimmered as he warmed to the topic.

"Blue topaz is quite rare. Most topaz is colorless but one like yours, with that magnificent pale blue color, is highly prized. Look at it. What do you see?"

He paused. With a nod, he went on. "You see the ocean and sky, both in one stone. Very special, for one gem to hold such power. Also, blue topaz is often called the stone of love, and is valued for the good fortune it brings its owner."

Tate shook his head in amazement. "You didn't tell me all of that when I brought it in."

The other man shrugged. "You did not ask. So will you be at the party at the school? I hear the children will be singing again this year."

He touched the brim of his hat. "We'll be there. I want everyone to meet Miss Channing."

Meg waved as they turned for the door. "Thank you, Mister Liu. I'll see you in a bit, then."

"My great pleasure, Miss Channing—on both counts." He smiled and bowed his head as they left.

The sun dropped low in the sky. Most shops were closing, and wagons, buggies, and horses headed toward the school. Foot travelers went that way, too. Some carried covered dishes while others brought garlands or wreaths.

He turned them toward where he'd left their buggy.

"We should get moving. The party will be starting, I reckon."

Meg nestled her head on his shoulder as they crossed the street. "I'm looking forward to meeting more of your friends. Everyone seems so nice."

He helped her step up and waited for her to settle into her seat. Then he went around and climbed in beside her. A twitch of the reins started them on their way. "Oh, we get some no-gooders now and again, but every town does. Mostly, though, Wylder's filled with decent folks. It's a fine place to live." He turned and placed a quick kiss on her cheek. "I'm glad you decided to make it home."

"Me, too."

Chapter 31

Meg's heart felt so full she could not keep a smile off her face.

Everywhere she looked, something or someone brought joy. They hadn't gone inside the schoolhouse yet and already she experienced more festivity than ever before. She had never attended a real party. The Reverend forbade such goings-on, calling them the work of the devil. Her mother had been too frightened to go against his wishes so there were no parties in their home.

One cannot miss what one does not know. Now that she saw how the rest of the world behaved, the pleasure they took in coming together to celebrate, she intended to attend as many festive occasions as possible.

She looked over at the man standing beside her. By far the handsomest in town, and he belonged to her—and she to him. It sent her mind spinning, but in a wonderfully delicious way.

"I never thought that you would end up living out here, Tate. When you asked after Violet and I told you she'd gone west, I really thought it would be a visit before you moved on."

The woman before them held a squirming toddler in her arms.

"I'm as shocked as you are, Miss Bloom. But then,

I didn't think I'd see you out here, either. And with a baby, besides."

"Well, surprises abound, don't they? And it's Missus Harvey now." She turned to Meg with a smile. "I'm looking forward to getting to know you. I'm Lily, Violet's eldest sister. I'm the one who told Tate she took the position as schoolteacher in Wylder. I guess you could say I nudged him out here." She laughed, a tinkling sound that stopped the child's wiggling. "We have a weekly sewing circle. Maybe you'd like to join us sometime?"

"That sounds delightful. I'd enjoy that very much, thank—oh!"

"Miss Channing? Are you all right?" Missus Harvey's voice sounded far away.

She couldn't have replied if she tried. Her throat tightened, her tongue dried up, and every rational thought flew from her mind.

"Meg?" Tate turned to look toward the street before he took a step in front of her and forced her to meet his gaze. "What's wrong? You look like you've seen a ghost."

Worse than a ghost. So much worse.

She nodded to the man who strode toward her.

"The Reverend."

And just like that, her contentment and sense of belonging were sucked away. The warmth in her heart turned to ice. She should have known better. He'd threatened to find her if she ran, told her there wasn't a place on earth or in hell where she could hide from him.

Strange, how he'd never mentioned heaven.

Funnier still, that these past days in Wylder had felt exactly how she imagined life past the Pearly Gates might be.

Not amusing at all, though, how the most joyful of moments could be stolen in a heartbeat.

She should have murdered him when she had a chance. Now, she'd rather kill herself than return to Boston with the man who stood before her with his hands on his hips and fire in his eyes.

The devil himself, come to take me back to hell, she thought.

Chapter 32

Tate spotted the two marshals near the road. It seemed they should have left by now but with the snowstorm and the holiday, who could blame them for lingering? Now he appreciated their presence.

He did not feel inclined to allow the man standing before them much leeway. One step out of line and he planned to knock the stuffing from the fellow. Then the marshals could do some good and return him to Boston—or hell, wherever they preferred so long as they kept him from coming near Meg again.

The Reverend. He'd been portrayed as such a monster that it seemed inconceivable that this skinny, pinch-faced ferret of a man could be the one who terrorized two women.

His fingers twitched. He fought the impulse to reach out and wrap them around the scrawny neck.

"Well, look at you." The man spat on the ground. "Dressed up like a harlot. What is that on your lips? Is that—good God, you're already painted!" He lifted a hand toward Meg's lips, but it never made it that far.

His wrist felt as thin as a bird's wing, all bones and air in Tate's grip. The impulse to squeeze surged inside him. One false move and he'd snap the man's wrist as easily as a child might crack a turkey bone.

"What the hell do you think you're doing? Get your hand off me!" The Reverend pulled his arm back, so he released him.

"Don't touch the lady." He didn't raise his voice.

In true Wylder fashion, a small ring of men stood to the side while others hustled the women and children into the schoolhouse. If he needed help, his neighbors would assist, although any of them alone could remove the interloper without fuss.

"Don't tell me what to do—and that's no lady! This is my daughter, and I'm taking her home to Boston." Spittle flew from his lips when he spoke.

Tate glanced at the woman who held his heart. Her eyes blazed, and she stood ramrod straight.

"You're not taking her anywhere. And if you know what's good for you, you'll turn right around and head on back the way you came." He opened his jacket button and pushed the sides back to reveal his gun belt. "Sooner rather than later."

The man's beady stare took in the guns. He reached into his breast pocket and pulled out a cigar. With a sneer he bit off the end and spit it out, struck a match he dug out of the same pocket, and lit up. It took a few puffs to get the fat cylinder going but it finally drew. The tip glowed bright red.

When Meg took a step back he looked over to where she stood. Her beautiful eyes flashed fear and in that instant he realized what caused the two round marks on her shoulder. The scars weren't fresh, but they were ugly enough to show that they'd come with pain.

Rage coursed through him.

"You filthy bastard!" He stepped in front of his beloved and shielded her from the man. "Leave or so help me God, I'll see you at the undertaker's before dinner is served."

A crude smile split the man's face and showed brown teeth. "Oh, that's how it is? I knew she'd be a harlot like her mother." He stuck his head to one side so he could peer around Tate's body. "She's not dead, you know. I let you think that, but she didn't die in the fire. Oh, no. I found her, too, the way I found you. And she came to no good, like I predicted. Living with a man down by the harbor, servicing him and refusing to come home with me."

"I don't blame her." The man's head snapped back but she went on. "Not one bit. I ran across the country with no money and no kin to get away from you. If I were dead I wouldn't go back with you. I hope she's happy and that the man treats her well because you sure didn't—and she deserves that, to have a good life with someone kind." She paused and placed a hand on Tate's arm. "There are good men in the world, I know that now. Go away, and never come back."

The man looked at her hand, then met Tate's gaze. His eyes narrowed and he took a long draw on the cigar before he spoke again.

"So you're the one who corrupted her?"

"Get out."

"You brought her to ruin? She's a harlot, you realize that, don't you?" Another long pull on the cigar. The end flamed bright red. "It's in her blood. Gets it from her mother, that worthless sinner."

"I plan to marry this woman so if you've half a brain in that disgusting little head of yours you'll keep your mouth shut." He swallowed the fury threatening to spill over. "Leave, if you know what's good for you."

"Is that a threat?"

"It sure as hell is. Now, go!"

Another pull on the cigar before he spread his arms to the crowd. "Did you all hear that? This man threatened me—me, a man of the cloth, no less. You're my witnesses!"

Tate watched as every man assembled slid his jacket back to expose his handgun. Those who weren't carrying curled fists. All looked ready to eat the intruder and spit him out in tiny, shit-sized pellets.

Defeat turned the Reverend uglier still. He looked at Meg, then glared at Tate.

"You can have her." He spat.

With a scowl he headed toward the road, puffing on the cigar so hard he left a cloud of foul-smelling smoke in his wake. He paused beside the stone wishing well and turned back before he raised his arm and tossed the cigar into the well.

"No!" Brantley, the U.S. Marshal, hollered as the man opened his fingers.

"Not in there!" The other marshal ran toward the well, then turned and ran back to the crowd. "Get down! Everyone get down!"

Men scattered. All except the Reverend, who stopped in the middle of the street and stuck his tongue out at the crowd.

A rumble came from within the wishing well.

Tate grabbed Meg and threw her down into a snowbank. He leapt on top of her and shielded her body with his.

The boom shook the ground, as if the center of the earth exploded. Snow undulated beneath them, like waves on the ocean. The sound was deafening.

He wrapped his arms around Meg's head and

prayed they'd live to see Santa Claus as dirt and debris showered them. A rock landed near his arm with such force it went through the snow and thudded on the frozen ground beneath.

That the marshals knew there were explosives in the wishing well meant only one thing: They'd dropped them in there. He figured they'd found his missing freight and, since they didn't get satisfaction on the gold claim and only managed to break a hand, they disposed of the explosives in a seemingly harmless way that would annoy no one but their owner.

He leaned back and gazed into Meg's eyes. "Are you hurt?"

Her bonnet lay crushed in the snow and she'd lost at least one hairpin but otherwise looked as beautiful as ever. She shook her head and managed a small smile.

"Did you mean what you said?" In a voice meant only for his ears, she murmured, "About getting married?"

He grinned. Here they lay, in a snowdrift, with debris from an exploded wishing well all around them, and she wanted to know if he intended to marry her. Who could understand the workings of the female mind?

"Every word. If you'll have me, that is."

She wrapped her arms around his neck and pulled him close. Her lips were inches from his when she nodded.

"I'll have you forever, Tate."

He kissed her and didn't care who saw them. They'd traveled long, hard roads to make it to this point and they deserved every bit of happiness life could offer.

It hit him then that the Christmas party waited for them, so he pushed up and helped his intended to her feet.

He glanced over his shoulder. No one seemed hurt by the explosion. Men were milling about, and a group stood near the hole where the well had been. Rocks and dirt dotted the snow in front of the schoolhouse.

In the street, the two marshals held the Reverend by the arms. It looked as if they'd gotten a man, after all.

"Can we still go to the party?" She retied the bonnet's ribbons and tucked a curl back into place. "I want to meet everyone."

"Of course, we can go." He brushed snow from her shoulders. "And I want everyone to meet you. This is our first holiday together."

He kissed her and when they broke apart she met his gaze. In that instant, nothing mattered but the woman in his arms and the future they'd have together. Everything that came before led them to this moment, this gift that brought two lonely hearts to beat as one.

She slipped her hand onto his arm as they walked toward the others.

"Merry Christmas, Tate."

"Merry Christmas, Meg." He leaned close. "By next year, I want that to be Missus Taylor."

She smiled up at him. "I want that, too."

A word about the author...

Sarita Leone loves happy endings—in life and on the page.

When she's not busy writing her next novel, this adventure-loving yoga teacher likes to hike, travel, and dance beneath the stars. She studies languages, enjoys making a mess in the kitchen, and never says "no" to fun.

Finding pockets of peace everywhere she goes, this author plans to make every moment of this journey count.